Writings
FROM
THE HEART

CANDICE UY CHAN

Writings FROM THE HEART

A Collection Of Narrative Poems, Lyric Poems, and Essays

ReadersMagnet, LLC

Writings From The Heart
Copyright © 2021 by Candice Uy Chan

Published in the United States of America
ISBN Paperback: 978-1-956780-57-4
ISBN eBook: 978-1-956780-56-7

All rights reserved. No part of this publication may be reproduced, stored in a retrieval system or transmitted in any way by any means, electronic, mechanical, photocopy, recording or otherwise without the prior permission of the author except as provided by USA copyright law.

The opinions expressed by the author are not necessarily those of ReadersMagnet, LLC.

ReadersMagnet, LLC
10620 Treena Street, Suite 230 | San Diego, California, 92131 USA
1.619. 354. 2643 | www.readersmagnet.com

Book design copyright © 2021 by ReadersMagnet, LLC. All rights reserved.
Cover design by Ericka Obando
Interior design by Mary Mae Romero

For My Husband, Kenneth,

And Our Daughters

Alexandra Elise and Margaret Kate

With Love

Part 1
THE EARLY YEARS

The Pretend Game

When I go to bed at night
With warm covers wrapped all tight,
I play pretend, my favorite game
And Mary Elizabeth is my name.

With long, curly locks of gold
Shining brighter than a penny of old,
And pretty eyes of cornflower-blue
Wouldn't you like that, too?

Lovely frocks of satin and lace
Oh! I wear them with such grace.
Silk stockings and dozens of buckled shoes,
I find it so hard to choose.

My dolly and I walk in the park,
Wearing finery as these is a lark.
And then a scrumptious afternoon tea
All laid out just for me.

Icing cakes on china plates
Oh! My tea is never late.
All too soon, it's time to go
How I wish it wouldn't hurry so!

When I awake and find just me,
I am as pleased as pie can be.
For though Mary Elizabeth may be my name
Playing pretend is just a game.

A Kingdom For Lost Things

If there were a kingdom for lost things
Which I hope there'd really be,
I know I'd find my ring
The heart-shaped one, such a pretty thing.

If there were a kingdom for lost things
Which I hope there'd really be,
I know I'd find the ball I lost
The one I threw a meadow across.

If there were a kingdom for lost things
Which I hope there'd really be,
I know I'd find my teddy bear
Oh! I hope he's none the worse for wear.

If there were a kingdom for lost things
Which I hope there'd really be ,
Why, I'd be sure to have a key
And keep it always safe with me.

The Cutty Sark, Queen Of Clippers

The Cutty Sark, Queen of Clippers
Proudly the seas she sailed,
Her white sails a-blowin' in the wind
The captain manning the tiller.

Through mighty gales and silent skies
She plowed on her ever-changing course.
Silks, spices, and gold she'd hold
From ancient India to the Golden Isles.

From starboard to port built she was,
Of gleaming timber and brass-bound oak.
On swiftest feet and lightest grace
A sight to behold she was.

Her glory days were soon cut short
Pirates swarmed the endless seas.
Days and nights of clanging swords
Echoing sounds of cannons' retort.

She sank beneath the blackened waves
Her sails burning and her timbers groaning,
The once majestic ship she was
Falling deep into a fathomless grave.

On a still and moonless night, they say
When gray mists blanket the Golden Isles
There, a looming shape they'd see
The ghostly clipper, remnants of her day.

Proudly the seas she'd sail once more
Her sails unfurled to catch the wind
The Cutty Sark, riding high
Queen of Clippers, part of our lore.

Sleeping

Sleeping
Has got to be my favorite thing.

Sleeping
I close my eyes without seeing.

Sleeping
Dreams flutter softly like butterflies' wings.

Sleeping
A state of blissful lying.

Sleeping
One of my favorite things.

Cups And Saucers

I love cups and saucers
I simply do!
And I know if you had one
You'd simply love them, too.

I have cups and saucers
Of many designs,
Some come with stars and moons
And some of pretty flowers all entwined.

I have cups and saucers
Capturing a palette's many hues,
Some are colored pink and green
And one mirroring the sky's endless blue.

I have cups and saucers
For tea parties and such,
All my cupboard friends
Like entertaining very much.

I have cups and saucers
Laid out side by side,
On my playroom's wall
They all reside.

I love cups and saucers
I simply do!
If you could see the many I've got
I know you'd simply love them, too.

Pillows

Pillows
So full and plump
That's how I like them most
Without all the lumps.

Pillows
So nice and fluffy
That's how I like them most
With all the squishy-squashy.

Pillows
So soft to lay my head upon
That's how I like them most
Gazing to the stars beyond.

Pillows
Let's start a pillow fight
That's how I like them most
Watching the goose feathers alight.

Our Cuckoo Clock

Our cuckoo clock always tells the time
Instead of a bird it has tinkling chimes
And when we hear them ring
We have to hurry everything.

At half past eight we are ready to go
The school bus is tooting its horn so
Bringing an apple, chalk, and slate
The cuckoo clock makes sure we're never late.

At half past three, we dash out of school
Waiting excitedly for our carpool
From the windows we lean to see
Hoping for a glimpse of afternoon tea.

At five into the shower we race
Precious minutes are not to waste
Learning lessons at our desk
Mother scribbling on our spelling test.

At seven we are a family
Seated for supper in harmony
Talk and laughter on the table round
The tinkling chimes a welcome sound.

At half past eight we're tucked in bed
Goodnight kisses on our heads
The cuckoo clock's hands of time
Another day is tomorrow, to rise and shine.

Strawberry Jam

I really like strawberry jam
I love it like no other!
I even like it better than ham,
Or gooey stuff like butter.

You see, it is my favorite treat
It's what I like the best!
More than any other sweetmeat
Strawberry jam can beat the rest!

I like it on my toast,
My pudding, my curds, and whey
Why I don't care much for roast,
Just strawberry jam anytime of the day!

I am as pleased as can be,
Strawberry jam trickling down my chin
You can see that it's me,
Flashing that toothy, red-mouthed grin!

The Honeybee

The honeybee is a busy bee
Flying all day from tree to tree

Hither, Thither,
Doesn't he ever get in a dither?

Darting from flower to flower
Single blossoms to heavenly bowers

The honey he gathers today
Will be saved for a rainy day.

My Secret Place

There used to be a place
Where I could just be me
Beneath the open sky
And miles of empty space.

Where the sweet-smelling grass abound
And gusts of breezes frolicked
Darting through the heavy boughs
To the cacophony of animal sounds.

The little brook gushing by
Splashing the children at play
Inviting me to lie on the bank
And stay for just a while.

This was long ago
When there was still a me
Now the place is nowhere to see
And even I am not who I used to be.

If I Were The Queen Of England

If I were the queen of England,
Everybody would at my command
Take blackberry and rye
And bake it into a pie.

If I were the queen of England,
Everybody would at my command
Take gooseberry, jam, and scones
And make them toppings for ice cream cones.

If I were the queen of England,
Everybody would at my command
Take jasmine and mint to stew
A most aromatic and lovely brew.

If I were the queen of England,
Everybody would at my command
A gallant knight or a fair lady be
All sit down and eat an enchanting tea.

The Heirloom Ring

It lies on my grandmother's hand
Wrinkled brown like the desert sand
Upon her finger it lingers
Softly, now and then with a shimmer.

It is an heirloom ring
More beautiful than anything
Fashioned of rubies and Spanish gold
It is a century old.

From Spain it came
To rest on America's Nevada plain
Stories and tales it has to tell
To one who has worn it well.

It has always been for the Chavez brides
A tradition they wear with pride
Every so often, grandmother says
It will be mine to wear on my wedding day.

Rainy Days

Rainy days are here to stay
Rainy days, my favorite days

I sit in my chair and watch the rain
Trickling down the frosted pane

I see the lightning strike the sky
Sending house mice scurrying by

Dark gray thunder booms and roars
Shaking trees to their very core

How I long to go outside in the rain
Running a bath beneath the drain

But I have to stay home instead
With thoughts of puddles in my head

Rainy days, do say you'll stay
And help me get my wish another day.

Spring

Spring is coming
Let's do a little swing
It's coming into town
Gaily bedecked in a flowered gown.

Bluebells are tinkling their chimes
Daisies dancing in rhyme
Fields shed their coats of gray
Spring is on her way.

Up in the sky so high
Blue Jays release happy sighs
Meadowlarks burst into song
Spring has been awaited for so long.

I skip, I hop, I dance
Perhaps I may see Spring by chance
And if she asks, "How do you do?"
I'll say, "I'm fine. I missed you, too."

Haircut

High up in the barber's chair I sit
I do not like it just one bit

Keep quiet and sit still I must
Fingers crossed that it's over fast

Snip, Snap, Snip
There goes a lock and a nip

I fidget, and squirm, and wriggle
To make the chair go jiggle-jiggle

Snip, Snap, Snip
More locks, a tuck, and a nip

I shut my eyes, afraid to see
The little girl that I would be

With a sweep and a flourish
He proudly declared, "I'm finished."

And my goodness did I preen,
At the lovely girl staring from the mirror scene.

Christmas

Christmas comes once a year
Friends and family all so dear

Yuletide logs and christmas trees
Never-ending stream of people there be

Snowflakes, fat and white, dropping by
Beneath the gray and black northern sky

Poinsettias red and holly green
Jack Frost silently creeps past unseen

Merry laughter and treacle jam
Popcorn strings and apple-roasted ham

Festive presents, in shiny foil and wrapper
What excitement and joy to uncover!

Christmas carols, young and old, we sing
Thanking God for this season's blessing.

God's Wisdom

He is wise
Who created the stars and skies
Painting strokes from dusk to dawn
Twilight glimmer of dancing fireflies.

He is wise
To have thought of roaring oceans
Sparkling brooks, churning seas,
And the sturdy redwood trees.

He is wise
To have planned desert sands
Birds, trees, and bees,
A long way beforehand.

He is wise
From black nothingness unseen
Craggy mountains and lush meadows
To verdant fields of valley green.

He is wise
I give all praise to thee
For without Him
There would not be a Me.

Clouds

Clouds
Gently rolling by
Lazily drifting
Across the great blue sky.

Clouds
Puffy white on a sunny day
Grayish black and bleak
Rainy days are here to stay.

Clouds
Young and old
Watching sunrise from the east
And twilight silently unfold.

Clouds
Tickled pink by the playful wind
So high, so high above,
Placed there by a hand unseen.

My Birthday Cake

Chocolate cake
Was what mother baked
Moist and brown
With trimmings all around.

Scalloped icing on the edge
Buttercream flowers deck the top
A little garden was what's about
And green frosting for its hedge.

Three layers high it was
Sticky marshmallow in between
Big and small chocolate coins
More than a cake ever has.

And most grand to see
Five bright candles in pink and white
For a little girl like me
It's the best birthday there'll ever be.

Breakfast

When I wake up
The sun's up and about
From the kitchen smells
Breakfast is ready, I can tell.

Bread, jam, and toast,
Applesauce, I like the most
Pancakes and waffles whose sauces
Like honey or maple are hard to choose.

Sunny eggs, ham, and crispy bacon
A heartier fare than I laid my eyes on
Freshly baked biscuits slathered with creamy, yellow butter
Which is it, the former or the latter?

A glass of milk or a sip of tea,
Whichever is fine by me
Cranberry juice or lemonade,
Cool to drink by the veranda's shade.

My Pet Dragon

I have a pet dragon
Whose name is Lap Seng
He came all the way from China
Where they grow ginseng.

He has eyes of emerald green
And his breath a ball of fire
With golden claws and golden scales
It makes for a very nice attire.

The ground trembles where he trods
His mighty wings like sails
A majestic creature he is
From horned head to powerful tail.

With me he is always gentle
His smoky breath stirring
He watches me into the night
As I lay in bed dreaming.

Sometimes I hear him croon
And heave a pensive sigh
I think it's because he misses
China and a time gone by.

Might he want to go home
So I thought to ask him one day
Lap Seng smiled a secret smile
And this is what he had to say.

Though I miss China and always will
My home is with you now, little miss
It is you I love above all
Not for a time long gone will I give up this.

I hugged him tight and kissed him sweet
With eyes of mist we turn to see
That's why I love my dragon very much
For Lap Seng is as fine a pet can be.

Thanksgiving Dinner

Roasted turkey, all golden brown
Mashed potatoes, gravy on its crown

Peas, carrots, and turnips on the side
A trail of honey on the slide

Beef stew and dumplings with bread
Soft and creamy butter for the spread

Apples, corn, and puddings sweet
Are an extra special treat

We bow our heads at the table
And say our prayers as best as able

A time for remembering is Thanksgiving
And thank Him for all His blessings.

Three Sister Witches

On the Isle of Bangor
Three sister witches live in a manor

Hilda is the eldest
White-haired, kind, and the shortest

Next in line comes Fay
Cheerful and sprightly all day

The youngest of them all
Patience, who is plump as a ball

Some days they work at their spells
Cauldron a-brewin' to make rain clouds swell

Day in, day out, they putter about
Figuring new things till they're out

With their wands and rhyming chants
They grant our wishes and our wants

Ever busy they are in the manor,
Hilda, Fay, and Patience of the Isle of Bangor.

Sorry

I am sorry
To hurt mummy so

When the words I said
Should have been kept instead

I am sorry
To hurt mummy so

I should have done my chores
Instead, I built sandcastles on the shore

I am sorry
To hurt mummy so

When I failed my spelling test
I could have done my best

I am sorry
To hurt mummy so

I hug her tight
And keep my face out of sight

She hugs me back
And kisses me tenderly
I'm glad everything is back as it should be
Between mummy and me.

The Old Attic Chest

In the attic I found a chest
Its hinges creaked with age
With yellowed paper and camphor balls
A trove of treasures laid to rest.

A lovely piece of paisley shawl
Gilded fan of embroidered lace
A pair of fine silver earrings
That some lady must have worn to a fancy ball.

A lovely crimson gown
Shot with threads of golden hue
Wouldn't it be fun
To wear such finery into town?

A cracked piece of looking glass
Silver brush and a silver comb
A dainty teapot set
Of elegant china and porcelain cast

Quietly I place them all back inside
These treasures that time has kept so fine
I watch them silently repose
In the old chest where they reside.

Christmas Day Years Ago

On the night the babe was born
Angels from on high blared their
Trumpets and blew their horns

Shepherds keeping watch that night
O'er flocks of sheep and little ewes
Were startled at the star so bright

The babe, on the manger he lay
His gentle breath stirring
Our Lord Jesus, asleep on the humble hay

The kings on camels brought their gifts
Gold, Frankincense, and Myrrh
For Him on blissful dreams who was adrift

On that night so long ago
When God sent down His infant son
We remember and thank Him so.

Despair

I do not understand me
I long to be let be
To let my tears come down in buckets
And cry my eyes out of their sockets.

If I Had Me A Boat

If I had me a boat
I'd set it downriver afloat

On it I will travel
Watching lands and mountains unravel

I'll have crabs, and shrimps, and dace
To make myself a superb bouillabaisse

I can wash my clothes on the River Nile
Soap bubbles following me mile after mile

And on summer nights I'd sit on the prow
Watching Nature put on her lovely show.

Summer Afternoon

The sun is warm on my head
Bumblebees fly lazily looking for flower beds
I race the gentle wind in a run
Chasing butterflies just for fun.

Happy Day

The sun is shining
The birds are chirping

I passed my grammar test
And in Arithmetic, I was proclaimed best

Aunt Peggy gave me a nickel and six dimes
For which I bought a nursery book rhyme

I had toy soldiers and milk toast for tea
And berry tarts as much as I can see

On the sweet, green grass I lay
Filling my nose with the scent of fresh-cut hay.

Naughty Sam

Sam has been naughty today
First he chewed my shoe
And then he spilled his milk
And dirtied the kitchen, too.

He barked and chased the birds
And our tabby cat, Marmalade
With her fur on standing end
Amber eyes hiding in the shade.

It was time to teach him a lesson
He deserves a spanking
Naughty Sam, naughty dog
For all his puppy prankings.

His head was downcast
His droopy ears hanging so
And in his eyes of golden brown
Such a look of woe.

My heart melted at the sorry sight
I gave him a talking-to instead
Sam yelped and ran in glee
And showered me with kisses on my head.

The Rich Man's Wife

The rich man's wife passes by
She is a lady of such class

With coiffed hair and jeweled studs
Strings of pearls and shoes of Venetian glass

Walking with her pet
She always makes quite a dash

A purebred poodle of white
On her neck a velvet sash

High and fancy, high and fancy,
They make the people stop and stare

The rich man's wife and her poodle pet
Walking the streets, such a likely pair.

Shadows

I lay on my bed
Watching the ceiling overhead
The funny shadows my hands have made
Into the gloom they start to fade.

Busy

I have to prepare for a test
And my room is just a mess
My unbound curls are all askew
Oh! How can the hours be so few?
I do not have a minute to waste
Everything has to be done in haste
If you can see how much I have to do
Won't you come and help me, too?

Hibernating

Deep in the lair he sleeps
All snug, and cozy, and toasty
The big brown bear.

Amidst autumn leaves of gold and red
Soft bark shavings, and fresh hard earth
The big brown bear.

He tosses, and turns, and sighs
Burrowing deeper in his homemade bed
The big brown bear.

Ripe cherries, and oh-so-sweet berries
And scores of sparkling rainbow trout
The big brown bear.

This seemingly endless napping
Is what they call hibernating
The big brown bear.

Flu

I had a fever
And a runny nose
My throat was sore and scratchy
Cold chills touching my toes.

Off to bed, mummy said
I'll have Doc come and see
So bundled up in bed I was
Waiting to see what was wrong with me.

He touched my forehead
And poked my ear
And nodding, he spoke to mummy
Saying words I could not hear.

So in bed I have to rest
Longing for the playing days of blue
You see, Doc had diagnosed
That I had caught the flu!

Puppy Song

Our precious little pup
Has learned a new puppy song

A yip, a yap,
And a bark two miles long

A whine, a croon,
And a rather shaky howl

He wanted to let us know
That he had lost his bowl

And now when we go to the park
We hear a yip, a yap, and a bark two miles long

There he sits chewing on his leash
Telling us he wants to tag along.

Our Street

Living on our street
Is really fine indeed
People come out each morning
With a smile to greet

Neighbors pass each other by
Bright hellos and cheery how-do-you-dos
Children darting in and out of yards
Playing Catch-Me-Quick and My-Oh-My

Our houses are all neatly in a row
Some with frilly curtains, one
A red-painted door, another with yellow walls
All put on quite a lovely show

If you happen to pass this way
I am sure you will
Our street is not hard to miss
Please come in and say you'll stay.

Have You Ever?

Have you ever wished
To be a princess
And live far, far away?

To stay at the castle top
Play with golden dolls
And silver balls all day?

Have you ever wished
To always wear pretty frocks
And sit upon a golden throne?

I think it would be lovely
To look around the kingdom at night
And have you call it your home.

Have you ever wished
To be a princess
And start it once upon a time?

Walking Down Fleet Street

Walking down Fleet Street
I heard a series of bleats
When I looked up
I had to pause for a quick stop.

A nanny goat was coming down the street
She, the one with the bleats,
Gleaming silver-white, the she-goat,
Head to foot in a flowered overcoat.

Elegantly shod in heels, her hooves,
Her hair swept in the latest pouf
Gloves, pearls, and a daisy hat
Have you ever seen a goat like that?

A most amusing sight, I tell you
Though you may believe it not to be true
Walking down Fleet Street one day
A nanny goat came my way.

Where The Children Go

At the first fall of snow,
The children get dressed, ready to go

Shrieking and laughing, they make a dash
Pattering boots hurrying in a rush

To the woods for a snowball fight
Lumps of white whipping by to their delight

Catching snowflakes with their tongue
Having them melt all around

Breathless fun from an afternoon well-spent
Gathering twigs for a makeshift tent

A mighty bonfire to ward off the chill
And ghost stories to add a shivery thrill.

So at the first sign of snow,
Follow their footprints and see where they go.

First Day

I must not be late
And I must remember to bring my slate
Pens, paper, and books already packed
My shiny red apple in the sack.

Our Mouse Fluffy

Fluffy
Is
Our
Pet mouse.

She lives in a
Sweet
Little
Yellow house.

She has snowy-white
Fur
And
Ruby-red eyes.

She is ever-polite
Has perfect manners
And is
Very nice.

She loves to play
Running here and there
Up
And about.

We love to sit
And watch her
Scurrying, head and tail
In and out.

A Day At The Farm

The dawn is coming
The night has gone into hiding
The birds are chirping
Red-combed roosters are crowing.

Cows in the barn start mooing
Geese a-flying and honking
Young ducklings learning their quacking
Goats joining with their bleating.

Farmer John wakes up yawning
Hurriedly, their breakfast he's preparing
Many chores to be a-doing
Better start while it's early morning.

An Evening Prayer

Dear Lord, as we prepare for bed
Let your angels fly overhead
Watch over us as we sleep
Give us dreams and slumber deep
Keep us safe from harm
Enfolded in your arms so warm
And when we wake at morn's first light
We thank you, Lord, for keeping us through the night.

I Have Seen The Wind

I have seen the wind
Playful and fun
Chasing the clouds away
Under the morning sun.

I have seen the wind
Blowing leaves nowhere to see
Gliding gently beneath
The soaring butterflies and honeybees.

I have seen the wind
Its laugh a soft caress
Darting in and out
The many folds of my dress!

Brushing

I like to brush my teeth
My little pink tongue
And the gums underneath.
I brush it up and down
Sideways, both ways
And then all around.
I toss a bit of floss
Nothing stuck in between
It sure adds an extra gloss.
I look in the mirror and smile
A line of gleaming crowns
Stretching to almost a mile.
The little girl I see
She takes good care of her teeth
As best as can be.

Raining

The rain is coming down quicker
And I am fast getting wetter
I should be going home sooner
It will be for the better.

Sleep, My Baby, Sleep

Sleep, my baby, sleep
Your father thru the hours
He will keep
Your mother, though the night be long
Watches by thee
With a cradle song
The birch leaves fall so gently
Like hushed dreams
Upon thy sweet head so silently
Sleep, my baby, sleep
Till the morn breaks
Crimson o'er the blackest night.

The Promise Of Fall

There's a nip in the air
A crisp, sharp bite
I push my hands, burrowing
Deeper, seeking comfort
In familiarity.

The trees have bared their souls
Having long shed
Their raiment
Scattered on the woodland floor
Scarlet, amber, and tones of gold.

Swirling haze of skittering leaves
Eager for this yearly demise
Breathing new onto the old
A promise kept
Redolent in the passing breeze.

Fire Upon The Hearth

I watch it on the hearth
From kindling and coal it sprang to birth.

The leaping flames leap high
Ambitiously wanting the velvet sky

Tongues of red dance in delight
Casting shadows from their flight

The teasing sparks hiss and turn
Vanishing, never to return

Merrily the flames take the chance
A sudden pop, a flickering glance

Before the brightness be doused forever
Leaving not even a glowing ember.

Make-believe Princess

Riding upon my horse
I lead it on a trot

Riding upon my horse
A princess I am not

Riding upon my horse
I pay the onlookers no heed

Riding upon my horse
I feel like a princess indeed

Riding upon my horse
I lead it on a run

Riding upon my horse
Playing make-believe is such fun.

Dancing Shoes

When I put on my
Dancing shoes
I feel
Light
And airy
I jump
I slide
I do a little tap
A twist here
A turn there
One graceful pirouette
I look down
And
See
I am back standing
On the ground
Again.

Homeward Bound

Today I am homeward bound
The train chugs softly along
Pillow-white smoke in their wake
The blowing whistle, a heartwarming sound.

I watch the miles go endlessly by
Landscapes with green-dotted trees
Rolling meadows of scattered sheep
Grazing under the serenely perfect sky.

Beyond the walls of stone
Where the sun kisses the morning dew
In the midst of my enchanted glade
Where I have come to stay, my home.

I have yearned to see it for so long
Its mellowed brick caressing my cheek
Warmth and Love echoing
The hypnotic strumming of a siren song.

The train slows in its tracks
Though the winds of Fate
May blow me near or far
My heart, my home, I'll always come back.

The Bride

There she stands
A most winsome and charming bride
A dainty wisp of a girl
All grown up from ribbons and curls.

In her gown of beaded white
A vision to behold she is
Behind her trails the train
Walking gracefully to the choirs' sweet refrain.

A draping veil
Of finest illusion tulle
Caressing a cheek blushed with rose
Beside her groom standing prettily, a pose.

Reverent whispers
And held-breath hushes
The bride, the bride,
Love and Happiness forever reside.

The Snow-bound Christmas Party

(Inspired by the story, The Snow Party, by Beatrice Schenk De Regniers)

All this happened on Christmas Eve
It is almost impossible to believe

What a snowy night that was
Flakes of white driven by friendly gusts

The bakery truck with its pies and rolls
Quivering jellies, plump puddings, and all

The cook with his platters of grapes and cheese
Glazed Christmas hams and stir-fried geese

Musicians on their way to the hall
That night there was to be a fancy ball

All got stuck in the deep, white snow
Leaving everyone nowhere to go

An idea soon sprang to mind
From those whose plans were left behind

We'll not let this weather dampen us so
Let's have a party, let's begin the show

All the neighbors came to see
And soon everybody joined in glee

What eating, and dancing, and partying
All around people were merrymaking

It was then we realized that the meaning
Is truly measured by the giving

The Christmas spirit was never truer that night
Truth be told, such a heartwarming sight

Though it has been many Christmas eves
Sometimes, I still find it impossible to believe.

My Adventurous Green Beret

I once had a green beret
On my head I could
Not persuade it to stay

It wanted to soar
Way up high above the trees
I guess it found my head quite a bore

It wanted to be seen
Blown by the wind down the streets
And asked by people where it had been

It wanted to be with the birds
Seeing for itself the many
Stories it had so often heard

It wanted to venture
Out into the great wide world
In search of adventure

So that was why it left me
I only hope my green beret
Is happy wherever it may be

So if you happen to see a green beret
Just try and talk to it
Perhaps you can persuade it to stay.

Sweet Sixteen

The clock is almost seven
And here I am not ready even

My hair is still up in curls
And I seem to have lost my pearls

My stockings are halfway up
And my shoes nowhere about

I don't have time to waste
I will be late if I don't make haste

The gown of finest needlepoint lace
That I must remember to wear with grace

My curls and pearls are now in place
Trembling fingers touch the shimmering necklace

Sparkling eyes and an enchanting smile
Pink-flushed cheeks in a while

I look in the mirror and preen
It's not everyday that I turn sweet sixteen!

Heaven To Me

I wonder what
Heaven
Will be like to me

Will it have
Silver fruits
On gold-laden trees?

Will there be
Rainbow dawns to fill
It all with light

Glorious days of Spring
And Summer, never to
Know the touch of a moonless night

Endless forests of redwoods tall
Vibrant flowers along
Placid waters of silver streams

Moving clouds of blue and white
So soft a pillow
Blissful on hushed dreams

I know this is what
Heaven will be like to me
For all the things that I love the most
He will let them be.

The Little Elf Princess

The little elf princess
She sits upon her throne
Made up of a silver thimble for a stool
And a piece of chewed-up bone

She sits all dressed up
In her pretty dress of spider's web
Holding a tiny wand in her hand
A broken piece from a pencil lead

She washes her face
With the dew from a morning glory
And then settles down to read a page
From someone's old story

The little elf-princess
She sits upon her throne
Beneath the speckled toadstool
The place she lovingly calls home.

The Secret Garden

The secret garden was what I'd been told
The flowers in the garden all sit down to chat
So one day I crept out to see
If it was what they were at.

"Good morning, Rose!" I heard Petunia say
"Did you sleep well last night?"
"Good morning to you and all," yawned the Rose
"I sure hope the sun comes out today."

"It's time to wash our faces"
Piped the Bluebells,
To which the Daisies laughingly replied
"And then we have to tie our laces."

"Don't forget to put on your bloom,"
Called the Daffodil,
"As if I have the space for that,"
Sighed the Marigold, "I'm running out of room."

"Hurry now, hurry now!"
The Violet said, "It will soon
Be time for folks to wake, and they
Mustn't see us, that we must not allow."

"I hate all this rush!"
Exclaimed the Lily,
"I lose all my things and
Now I can't find my sash!"

The honeybee hovered near
Bringing bits of crusty honeycomb
And sips of honeyed tea
"Bless you, our darling dear!"

Then it became quiet all around
The folks were now about
And the morning sun rising up
Not a peep was heard from the garden ground.

This will be our secret, you and me
Tiptoe down to the gardens on early morns
Be still and you must shush
And all I told you, you will see.

The Greatly Misunderstood Spider

Spiders
I think
Are misunderstood creatures.

Why
Is it
That they usually appear in horror features?

With
Hairy legs
Huge eyes, and a nasty bite, they don't exactly endear.

Why
Miss Muffet
Was very frightened to have one sit so near!

But
Spiders are
Very industrious, weaving intricate webs of various designs.

So
Beautiful and
Awe-inspiring, even to us humankind.

They
Are very
Clever, too, catching flies and gnats with their web,

Or
Dangling silk
Like a bait, jumping anything with that spun thread.

Of course
We think
That drinking blood is so cruel,

But
We can't
Really expect spiders to survive on gruel.

Spiders
I think
Are really misunderstood creatures,

But
It is
Because we don't understand that it's their nature.

The Pony Cart

The pony cart comes to a stop
Outside the small grocer's shop

Oh! What goodies there are to see
Especially to one such as me

There are brown potatoes for a pound
And sacks of corn in a mound

Fleshy turnips and fresh red beets
Sweet whole pickles and cheesecloth sheets

A bucket of lard and lumps of butter yellow
Bolts of muslin and kegs of cider mellow

Clanking sound of pots and pans
Finely crafted lace made by hand

And lastly in a large old tin
Maple sweets, toffee, and peppermint creams

All these to my heart's delight
When the pony cart comes into sight.

The Mermaid's Wish

The little mermaid
She lives under the vast blue sea

With shining eyes and oysters on her tail
She is as pretty as can be

She likes to spend her time
Drawing pictures on the sand

Imagining things as she might see them
If she could go walk on land

Sometimes she sings herself a song
Or chase the little fishes for fun

She does think and wonder, too
How it feels to play under the sun

Oh! Little mermaid wouldn't it be nice
If you and I could just get some advice

You could be me, and I could be you
For just a day, wouldn't that be lovely to do?

My Secret Diary

My diary is a secret book
I keep so many things in it
If only you would care to look

I wrote the date of my first cry
I had scraped my knee
And cried my eyes till they were dry

It tells of my favorite gurgling brook
And passing reading time
Down in the kitchen, my little nook

March was when I had my cat
And the month after that
I got my very first flowered hat

My secret list is very long
And my prized badges
From the Brownie Club where I belong

It will always be full of writings
Whether the day comes bringing
With it good or bad tidings

And when the sun has gone away
I put my diary back down
Tomorrow is yet another day.

Afternoon Tea Party

The nursery clock rings at three
I rush in from play
To find my tea all laid out for me

There's gooseberry and raspberry tarts
Oh! So plump and juicy
Sugar-dusted cookies shaped like hearts

Light and fluffy jelly rolls
Like lovely snowflakes they melt
And candied maple in coconut balls

Butterscotch brownies and cream-filled scones
And oh to my delight
Scoops of ice cream on an ice cream cone

Cucumber sandwiches and royal icing cupcakes
And in the center of them all
A pink and white chocolate cake

Party hats, crackers, and balloons, oh how grand!
It's my first birthday tea party
This must be the finest in the land!

Bathtime

When the clock chimes at six
I rush down the garden path

Straight into the bathroom
Ready for my bath

I watch the water filling
As I lay back in the tub

Giving chase to the soap suds
As I give my body a good rub

Splish, Splosh, Splash,
Sailing away with my rubber duck

The water sprays all around
And ducky gives a happy quack

Soon it's time for drying
And I'm tied up in my terry robe

Then it's time for bed
Listening to bedtime stories from of old.

Four Seasons

The coming of Spring
New life! New breath!
In every flowering plant and flower
The promise that Spring brings.

On playful feet comes Summer
Sandy shores and long-stretched
Days of endless blue
Gayest, frolicking-fun weather.

Nimbly on lightest tread is Fall
Woodland animals in a hurry and rush
Vivid skies of orange red
Answering to the wild geese's call.

Best of all is Winter
Miles and miles of whitest snow
And heartwarming hearth-fires
The loveliest season ever.

PART 2

THE INTERVENING YEARS

Play Our Song Again

Play our song again
The one playing that November night
When I first met you then

The words so much sweeter
Your hand clasped in mine
I draw your body nearer

Its melody lingers long in the air
Like the jasmine scent
Intangible, but its presence always there

Our bodies gently sway to the motion
Even after all this time
Love remains a potent emotion

Resting my cheek against yours
Drawn by your stirring breath
Rhythmic cadence on the dance floor

I look into your eyes
In its radiantly gleaming depths
I see startling and adoring surprise

Enfolded in your tight embrace
In you, my love,
I have found my place

Play our song again
And this time
Let there be no end.

The Owl

She flies the expanse of sky
Gazing sharply at everything with a beady eye

On greater heights she soars
A passing blur beneath the waterfalls' roar

She glides and slides on the wind
A mighty shadow of white unseen

A creature shrouded in mystery and fear
Dark and forbidding tales we hear

She brings the day's bountiful catch
Her young inside the eggs already hatched

A juicy moth or a tiny field mouse
A wayward vole or a wood grouse

She settles down for a well-deserved rest
Ensconced with her brood in the nest.

Faith

She sits alone in the pew
To those unawares
She is but one of a few

She makes the sign of the cross
In the name of the Father
The Son and the Holy Ghost

The fingers move on weathered beads
Lifting her face
She tells Him of her needs

Prayers spring forth with ease
From her mouth
The slight movements never cease

Oh! To have Him hear her plea
She walks the center aisle
Suffering silently on bended knees

She stares at his bloodied face
Hoping to be filled
With His abundant grace

She wipes the wound at his side
Where the Roman soldiers struck Him
Blood flowing freely to slide

The look of adoration
Lighting her humble face
Startling in its complete devotion

Oh! To have this woman's faith
This vanishing trait
We will do well to imitate.

Weep No More, My Lady

Weep no more, my lady
Of true love that has yet to come

Play no sorrowful tune
Upon that melodious harp

Let thy eyes not despair
Thy fragile hands of torment bind

No pain burden thy loving heart
Thy steps not falter on the rough-hewn path

Keening cries of suffering be unheard
From parched lips of ashen-gray

Sing of moonlit forests and twilight love
Upon that melodious harp

Thy eyes be agleam with laughter
Thy fragile hands a sweet caress

Let love flourish in thy loving heart
Thy steps steady to a loved one's cadence

Joyous cries come forth be heard
From sun-kissed lips of trembling red

Weep no more, my lady
For true love will come thy way.

You Have I Loved

You have I loved
When the twilight meets the dawn
When his darkness touches her warmth

You have I loved
When the crashing surf and the pounding sea
Lay open their souls upon the restless sand

You have I loved
When the lonely cliffs and the whispering moors
Stand strong and tall against the icy winds

You will I love
From amber days to purple nights
A trace of love lingering still

You will I love
When the sea no longer touches the sand
Unceasing and infinite this love

You will I love
Though death will part our ways
Grief and sorrow, in its cold, inconsolable embrace

You will I love
For lasting and always
Have I loved you.

Lilies Are For The Dead

Lilies are for the dead
Was what grandmother said
On that cold and rainy day
When Father was laid to eternal rest

A little child I was
Unknowing of the chasm between life and death
I knew only of crying
Unending sorrow in my heart

A myriad of people in black
Veiled faces rimmed in grief
The earth soft and moist beneath us
Father was to lie there forever

The old priest murmured a prayer
Seeking peaceful repose for a departed soul
Two forlorn figures in black
My grandmother and I

A handful of earth
Coming to rest on the black coffin
A pure white lily, trembling,
Stark against the somber gloom

Once again we stand alone
My grandmother and I
Our faces shaped by the passing of years
Life shining undimmed in our eyes

I lay the lily upon the silent grave
My mind searching a distant memory
Lilies are for the dead
Grandmother had once said.

Musings In A Graveyard

I walk along
My restless footsteps
Stirring the fallen leaves

My fingers lightly touch
Marbled tombstones faded
With the passing of time
Names of people who had lived
Worn by age and decay

It lies in veiled silence
Stately trees guard their eternal repose
Whispers carry on the passing breeze
A gentle father, working hands
A laughing mother, font of love and warmth

How many have lain here
For far too long, forgotten and lonely
How many were once a beloved
The pride of a family
Now laid to rest forever

The lives they had lived
The people they have touched
Here, among the weeping willows

They come for eternal slumber
Their ashes carried by the wind

I walk along
My silent footsteps
Stirring the fallen leaves.

Crush On You

I do not know what it is that I feel
All I know is that I want you near

The way your beautiful black eyes
Crinkle in merriment and laughter

The sound of your voice
Sends me humming through the day

My thoughts scatter like ashes
Your very nearness makes me breathless

I long to touch your strong hands
My fingers tremble with the need

How can you not read my eyes
The lonely beating of a heart

I love you, I know I must
I have never felt this way before

I only hope that someday
You would feel this way for me, too.

Regret

I stare
Unseeing at the
Tattered remnants of a lonely life

The gray clouds
Gathering, the overcast skies
A coming storm

A staccato of footsteps
Stiff, stilted words spoken
On gray-pallored lips

A desperate, beseeching glance
Love burning fiercely in his eyes, undimmed
Blind fool I was

Pride held me back
The footsteps faded in the storm's onslaught
And the door swung close, forever

Forty years have passed
Bitterly cold embers
In Pride's unconsoling embrace

Deep, harsh sobs
Wrack the frail body
Pained lines on the face

How late to realize
So much to regret
That I have always loved you.

The Long Walk

I walk deep in the snow
My thoughts on seasons long ago

The sharp wintry air
Bleak on a landscape bare

River trails course weathered cheeks
A refuge I try to seek

Where once was you and I
Now the whisper of a solitary sigh

No surcease for this pain
Time a soothing balm in vain

Longer I walk in the snow
Echoing thoughts of long ago.

The Singing Bone

(inspired by a German fairytale, as collected by the Grimm Brothers)

There is a tale I've been often told
About a singing bone centuries old

A sad tale this be
A lesson to be learned you'll see

Once two brothers set out
A wild boar they sought to rout

If the creature he happened to slay
The king's daughter his bride that very day

The younger smote the rampaging boar
Over the hills his resounding battle roar

But Envy and Malice ruled the elder's heart
And he made Death do them part

Claimed the wild boar as his own
The king's daughter he won

Buried for years beneath the sand
Under God's all-encompassing hand

One day, a shepherd who was alone
Chanced upon a piece of white, buried bone

He put it to his mouth to play
And heard what the bone had to say

Most troubled he was at all this
Telling his king something was amiss

When the King heard the bone start to play
The ugly deed was brought to the light of day

The elder brother, he soon breathed his last
In the clutches of Death he was held fast

A proper burial was given to he
Befitting the fallen warrior he be

In peaceful rest he now lay
Justice served to him on that day

So ends the tale of the singing bone
No more it sang that mournful tone

'Tis a tale that I've been often told
One that is centuries old.

Sleeping Beauty

(inspired from the fairytale collection of the Grimm Brothers)

The people tell of a princess long ago
When kings and princes once ruled so

Sleeping Beauty was her name
For Beauty and Goodness she was famed

Eyes of sapphire-blue and sun-kissed hair
Praises were sung for she, most wondrous fair

How could anyone foretell
The tragedy that was soon to befell

For upon her an angry fairy heaped a curse
As she lay in the arms of her nurse

On her sixteenth birthday she shall prick her finger
In endless sleep she shall linger

Only then will she wake from love's first kiss
And in her true love's arms find lasting bliss

The sad day soon came to pass
Grief and gloom over the castle was cast

The good fairies then cast a spell
Endless sleep for the people who loved the princess well

Entangling vines and climbing ivy hid the tower
The Sleeping Beauty underneath the rose bower

For years and years 'twas hidden from view
Tales of the sleeping princess so grew

Kings and knights sought an entrance to gain
Alas! Their most gallant efforts were in vain

Then one day came a young king
The good fairies guided his mighty swing

Thick vines and ancient ivy fell before his way
And in his heart surged hope so gay

Upon such enchanted loveliness he was greatly stirred
That sweet a kiss, her eyes fluttered

Soon there was great rejoicing over the land
In marriage he took her hand

And happily they lived thereafter
Fathering many a son and a daughter.

Snow White

(inspired from the fairytale collection of the Grimm Brothers)

Once there lived a queen
Long had she yearned
For a baby daughter to wean

With hair of deepest, darkest night
Lips of ruby-red blood
And skin to rival that of fairest light

Granted was her heart's desire
How everyone was gladdened and rejoiced
However this time was but a while

Death soon came for the queen
A chill upon the castle
As though by a hand unseen

In another, the king hoped to find solace
Love and care for his daughter
Who'd never known of a mother's embrace

The stepmother's beauty well hid the evil within
A witch of blackest magic
Her stepdaughter's demise she was planning

A rose in bloom, Snow White grew
Arousing the queen's jealous heart to no end
Like the most potent of her poisonous brew

For none to compare as fairest of all
The queen tasked the royal huntsman
To bring about Snow White's fall

Bring her heart to me
And you shall be greatly rewarded
Whatever your heart's desire be

The huntsman went to do as bid
But his love for the princess
Compelled him to halt the deed

Weeping, he fell on his knees
Telling her of the queen's evil plan
Hurriedly into the forest Snow White flees

The woodland animals helped in her flight
Taking her to the tiny house
Where the seven dwarves took pity on her plight

While the dwarves worked in the mine
Sewing clothes and keeping house
Snow White spent to while away the time

But all was not well
For the wicked queen found out
Snow White was alive and where she dwelt

Transforming herself to her raven's surprise
She became a toothless old hag
Such a clever disguise!

She went to the cottage by the clearing
Offering the Apple of Death
In exchange for water from the nearby spring

At that first bite
Snow White fell into eternal sleep
And the queen quickly took flight

The seven dwarves chased her down
Shrieking, she fell off the cliff
Her broken body lying on the ground

They laid Snow White in a glass coffin
By her side all day and night
They kept watch on the princess within

Then one day Prince Charming
Astride his mighty steed
With its glossy mane tossing

He had come from far away
Hoping to catch a glimpse
Of the princess he had heard people say

His heart stirred with love
A kiss he pressed upon the pallid lips
Snow White's eyes flickered to look above

She was again filled with life's glow
As with that kiss
Her breath did it bestow

He carried her off to be his bride
To that faraway land
Where happy endings reside.

Philippe, The Gay Duke Of Orleans

Philippe, the gay Duke of Orleans
Was already known as such
Even way before his teens!

He loved the light and buttery french toast
Rather than feast on the
Huge platters of greasy pig roast.

He dressed in velvet bows and satin ties
Many a lady did he outdo
Knowing him, it was no surprise.

Philippe would rather primp and coif his wig
Than sit with the belching knights
Raising wine goblets for a swig.

The ladies found him so fancy
How they loved him
He was such a dandy!

With feathers, hats, and a powdered face
What a sight he was
The courtiers could only say, "what a waste!"

He amused to no end the king's court
For all his antics, Louis gave his
Brother a most unladylike snort.

He'd rather dance a waltz on the marble floor
Than be out in the battlefield
Laying his life before death's door.

How proper he was of his manners
The talk of politics and war
Gave him the chills and the shudder.

If only Philippe had been born a girl
Do you think it possible
That he could have invented the twirl?

You must agree, he is a most fascinating subject
Though I'm sure many in his time
Would say, "non!" and object.

What a funny, unbelievable story
And to think I learned it
From the annals of history!

The Tragedy Of Queen Marie Antoinette

She was Louis the XVI's wife
And is best known
For her pampered and extravagant life.

Queen Marie Antoinette was her name
Upon her pretty head the
French Revolution is quick to blame.

She was a lady of impeccable style
Sipping scented tea and indulging in
Idle chatter all the while.

How she loved gowns and trinkets and such
Only the finest silks and pearls
Upon her skin would touch.

Louis loved her to distraction
And he built Le Petit Trianon
For her amusement, a most luxurious mansion.

Into it much money was spent
And down the drain
The hard-earned people's money went.

From her lofty seat of cocooned security
She cared not a whit
For France who was deeply mired in poverty.

Till the mobs took it upon their hands
Working day and night
To come up with an elaborate plan.

Started the revolution they did
Ousting the members of royalty
From where they hid.

But it was Marie Antoinette they hated
For the gossips and plain folk
Had heard of what she said.

"Let them eat cake!"
Set to festering their wounds so sore
This insult they could not take.

And so she was charged with treason
And a mock trial soon set
For her execution.

Marched she was to the guillotine
Down and swift came the blade
Her head rolling into the basket for all her sins.

Louis the XVI, too, had his date
As her weak and useless husband
He was doomed to share her fate.

For Marie Antoinette and her king
The bells of justice
Tolled a deafening ring.

Daughter Of England

Victoria was only eighteen
When she ascended to the throne
Of England and became its queen.

On her coronation day
The scepter in her hand and
Upon her head St. George's crown lay.

She said to herself, "I will be good."
And then set out to do the
Things few would have expected she could.

Descended from the line of Hanover
She never saw herself as weak
Nor ever felt hindered by her gender.

Conquering India she rose
A great and mighty nation
To be reckoned with across the coast.

With ivory and diamonds from the mines
Queen Victoria's wealth
Increased a hundredfold in no time.

Under her long and successful reign
Came the three countries
Known as Scotland, Ireland, and Great Britain.

Responsibly did she heed her call
Keeping England
Well abreast of all.

Her enemies before her knelt and bowed
In Queen Victoria's presence
They were properly cowed.

And after sixty four long years
Peaceful rest at last her reward
With her beloved Prince Albert forever near.

Now we only recognize her in the portraits of Winterhalter
Sitting upon her elegant throne
A picture of grace and solemnity, England's beloved daughter.

Elizabeth, The Virgin Queen

She was the daughter of Ann Boleyn
And never dreamed
That one day she would be queen.

This headstrong daughter of Henry the VIII
A woman she may be
But truth be told, she was no waif.

Possessed of a heart so bold
Feisty courage and a fierce temper
In her courtly garb, a sight to behold.

With hair of flaming titian-red
Piercing, knowing eyes of shrewdness
And shaved eyebrows high on her head.

It was she who said
"If I am a woman, then I
Have the heart of a man instead."

During this her reign
Many sought to topple her
So England's throne they could claim.

She sent them to the Tower of London
There they met their demise
No one granted her mercy nor her pardon.

Even her cousin, Mary, Queen of Scots
Though of kith and kin
Spared from death she was not.

Accused of the highest crime, Treason
Because of this
Mary was sentenced to die by execution.

Splendid in warfare
How England flourished and prospered
Under her care.

Spain found out too late
That this sharp-tongued virago
Could be as hard as slate.

Her well-armed schooners and clippers
Sank the Spanish Armada
Sinking rapidly beneath the waters.

Beloved queen of her country
Nevertheless; there must have
Been times when she was lonely.

Because through it all
She had no Prince Consort
Only courtiers at her beck and call.

How strange that she never married
That is one question
Scholars have long studied.

But you must understand
For a woman of her time
The sacrifice that must be made for the land.

For Elizabeth, the Virgin Queen
England was her king
And nothing could ever come between.

Courtship

He has come calling
Mustering all his courage
He had taken the first step
But still the task seemed daunting.

He rings the bell
His collar suddenly seems too tight
He fidgets and brushes his hair, once too many
Could she be home, he couldn't tell.

Her mother opens the door
Gives him a knowing smile
Making him flush to his ears
How he wishes to be swallowed by the floor.

She leads him to the living room
He stands ramrod straight like the grandfather clock
And wonders if he is
Playing to perfection the role of a petrified groom.

Finally, she is here!
Oh, divine! What sweet bliss!
To have his dream girl
Standing by so near.

Mother leaves them alone
Saying she has to go
To the kitchen and make
Use of the phone.

He gives her the single rose
"I hope you like it," he says.
"Thank you," she replies and blushes prettily
Holding the flower to her dainty nose.

His heart skips a beat
His arm itching to be
Placed around the back
Of her seat.

They sit some more, talk, and laugh
Sometimes they run out of words
So to break the silence
He pretends to cough.

She gives him lemonade
He gulps three glasses in a row
Feeling he'd been running out too long
And in desperate need of shade.

The clock is chiming at four
He stands, upsets his chair,
And almost topples the empty glass
Fumbling the lines he has rehearsed before.

The words he struggles to speak
He stammers and stutters
Tripping over his tongue
Until it comes out in a squeak.

"May I call on you again?"
Her cheeks peony-red, the
Look in her eyes dreamy
"I will see you then."

He goes out the door
His feet on angel's wings
Barely touching the suddenly
Non-existent floor.

She dashes straight to her room
Whoops, shrieks, and flings herself
Upon the bed, holding to
Her nose the rose, a picture of love in bloom.

 Psycho

(inspired from the novel by Robert Bloch)

The scene is one humid afternoon
In a tiny, sparsely furnished room

The couple lying on the bed
Their voices mingling with the fan overhead

This relationship, her life seemingly going nowhere
Life just sometimes is not fair

She hurriedly dresses to get back to work
Settling into a routine familiar as clockwork

Her boss arrives with bragging client in hand
Presenting her cold cash to keep, forty grand

The crisp, green bills as dark as sin
Tantalizing subconscious thoughts from within

For safekeeping in the bank, her boss says
She replies yes, but in her mind plans a getaway

Tossing luggage and passport in the car
This new adventure had once seemed so far

Her conscience-stricken and guilty thoughts
By endless driving, peace could not be bought

The heavy rain, upon her windshield it lashed
In the distance she saw a blinking flash

The Bates Motel, it read
Shelter for the night, perhaps some food and a warm bed

Marie Samuels, she signed her name
Norman, Norman Bates, he said was his name

He gave her the keys to room number one
To prepare coffee and sandwiches, off he was gone

The woman's voice carried on into the room
Its grating harshness breaking through the darkening gloom

Norman appears in the room to say,
"I'm sorry, mother isn't herself today."

After some talk, they called it a day
Dark, torturous thoughts he could not hold at bay

She undressed in the now-famous shower scene
The picture frame moves from where it's been

His eyes staring at her from behind the wall
At her blatant nudity framed by the waters' fall

The shower curtain is suddenly thrust aside
The look of horror on her face as he steps inside

The knife is raised high into the air
With each downward thrust, onto skin so bare

Her endless scream seared into our brain
Like her blood, mingling with water down the drain

For Norman was his mother
There couldn't have been any other

While in the basement her corpse rotted on the rocker
Their personalities existed in one another

Truly a classic masterpiece of its time
Insanity and terror, its mix sublime

What an impact it has on us all
On the many women who refuse to enter the shower stall

Psycho is the name of the film
Directed by Alfred Hitchcock, who else but him?

Killing So Softly

Strangler claims latest victim
Read the newspaper's headline as I passed the street scene

I quickly make the sign of the cross
As the busy street I hurried across

What is this town coming to
I shake my head to rue

Month after month it's almost the same
Unsolved stranglings, still no one to blame

We don't go out late at night
Safely in our homes by the sun's last light

We're told to keep our senses keen
But still the strangler lurks unseen

The victims give all their trust
Hardly a trace of struggle in the dust

It must be someone we know
In the town, suspicion and mistrust now grow

The old timers would say remember when
Twenty years ago it had happened then

The same pattern, the same method
All eight stranglings, gone unsolved

I was just fourteen
A growing girl with a mother for kin

Father had left us that summer
Saying he loved us no longer

When the stranglings started
Mother and I clung to each other, afraid to be parted

Fear sowed its seed in our town
All joy and spontaneity died down

Eyes darted in fearful silence
Our hearts beating an irregular cadence

As suddenly as it came
The strangler ended his game

Leaving no clue to remind
Of the tragedy that was left behind

Save for a cashmere scarf
Lying on a pile of leaves, dwarfed

That evidence so carelessly thrown
No conclusion from it was ever drawn

And now it has started again
Happening as it did way back when

I now tremble in fear
For I, too, have a daughter I hold most dear

I remember those nights too well
When mother would sit frozen as though by a spell

Eyes ablaze in maniacal glee muttering
Disjointed phrases and drool dripping

Twisting the cashmere scarf in her hands
Moonlight gleaming dully on her wedding band

How she approached them with stealth
And watched them gasp their last breath

I wish only to forget
The past so I can live without regrets

The summer wind suddenly turns chilly
And I wrap the cashmere scarf tighter around me.

Autumn In My Heart

The leaves are brown and gold
The wind has a touch of coldness
My footsteps walk softly
Lost in the carpet of leaves

How does one search for a lost love
A love unfaded with the passing of years
How do I forget the nuance of your smile
The warm cheek, so soft against mine

The limpid gaze as the
Curtain lifts from the sedan chair
How does one forget
The warmth of your hand upon this cold heart

I can only weep
Thinking of those happy years
Fate, in its twists and turns
Has not blessed this love

All around
The leaves swirl upon my feet
I remember the scent of you
Washing over me in painful memories

I lift these tear-filled eyes to the sky
This lonely heart, these aching steps
This endless autumn
Never to give way to Spring.

Love From Afar

The moon shines brightly tonight
It touches the lake's surface
I see the reflection of us

The night wind blows gently
Rippling across the willows
Slowly, you fade away

I stretch my hand to touch, to grasp
Clutching at nothingness
Only warm remembrances linger

The stars beautiful in their brilliance
Hang silently in the sky
This forlorn figure, alone

Past regrets, unforgotten thoughts
Should I have let you go
Should I have not yielded to our apparent Fate?

To only love you in this lifetime
Loving you from afar
How our love must be.

Don't Wait For The Night

Don't wait for the night
To speak to me of your love

Don't wait for the night
To run your fingers through my hair

Don't wait for the night
To look upon me with your loving gaze

Don't wait for the night
For us to meet beneath the silent oaks

Don't wait for the night
For the darkness to enfold us

Don't wait for the night
For it is far too long

Don't wait for the night
Lest my love for you drift out of sight.

Missing

(Dedicated to the memory of the Missing Children in America)

Where have the children gone
People ask to this very day

Playing out on the streets
Off on the way to school

Walking back to their homes
Or just at the corner store

Suddenly to vanish into thin air
As if they had never been there

No one to see, no one to hear
The terrified eyes and silent screams

What evil lurks behind
The seemingly pleasant streets

What lies beneath the charm and smile
Their minds of dark and twisted intentions

Where have the children gone
To this day no one can say

Their families in anguished grief
Tremble in sadness and clutch at dwindling hope

Pictures on the walls remain
Of their innocent, carefree smiles

Years and years have passed
Only their memories left behind

To this very day the cry remains
Where have the children gone

In The Quiet Woods

In the quiet woods of winter
I walk on deep white snow
Somewhere, a gray owl calls
Answered by sleigh bells' chimes

Pristine mist surrounds me
Deep thoughts of welcome intrusion
Of people who travelled this path
Snowprint on snowprint, nearer and nearer

One imprint makes all the difference
For anyone who has ever been this way
Forging trails of immaculate white
Snowprint on snowprint, ever nearer

Longer still I walk the unseen
Snowflakes drifting down so softly
Gently blanketing in its wake
My footprints on the snow.

To Be In Love

I wish to be in love
A love of blooming rapture
And yellow-shaded breezes
A love gaily bedecked with joy

I wish to be in love
A love of murmuring springs
And walks along the byways
A deep-seated, contented love

I wish to be in love
A love of gentle seas
And glowing stardrops
A love of calm tranquility

I wish to be in love
A love to embrace all
And transcend mortality
A love for all eternity.

Blessed Be Green Gables

(inspired by The Anne of Green Gables books by Lucy Maud Montgomery)

The carriage climbs the curving road
To towering oaks and lombardies
Youthful flowers flushed from Spring
Dotting the landscape so serene

Farther down, the little house stands
Seats of silence outside the door
Fresh curtains hanging from the sill
Warmest sight to one so dear

Sunlight streaming through shutters white
Splashing rays on walls of chintz
Rippling waters cast on the shining lake
Singing by so sweet green grass

On that June day long ago
When I was five and six
This first sight of splendid glory
Rushed memories so deeply moving

The years have swiftly passed
Faint echoes of the distant past

Beautiful days still linger though
Unchanging with the seasons

A blessed font of love sincere
Beacon of everlasting light this be
Behold my heart and my home
Blessed be, Green Gables, blessed be.

My Yearbook

One day at a loss
My yearbook I did come across
And on its old and yellowed pages
I found the me of the ages

The smiles on the faces
Made me think of all the phases
When we were put to the test
But mostly when we did our best

Victory was ours to hold
A fitting accolade for one so bold
And we set out to sail
Leaving behind us a trail

And so we blazed high and far
Reaching our dreams by ship, rail, and car
Till we become what we are now
As has always been our vow

But Summer cannot stay for long
Winter came and sang her song
And now that I am old and gray
I bask in the memories of those glorious days

And so one day yearning to find
The me that I had left behind
I peeked into the pages bound
And I who was lost am now found.

Curtain Fall

Velvet curtains silently fall
Sound of applause; this
Beautiful face, this honored name

Cascading roses gleaming
Blood-red against the harsh light
Kissing lips a-trembling

Eyes of eloquent truth
Soaring spirit on endless flight
This bright star, glistening tears quivering.

Waves

Waves gently at the shore
Crests of foaming white
Sunlight on the water
Brilliant colors, a shimmering kaleidoscope

Soft white sand shifting
Swirling patterns on the breeze
Pebbles glowing with translucent fire
Lying cradled beneath the sky

Ripples darting in silence
Echoes of the mighty sea
Murmurs play on hidden strings
Everything a picturesque serenity

Light so swiftly chasing away
Shadows touching placid waters
Moonbeams rushing out to play
Peaks of white unending.

The Promise

The moon has risen high
As I step the well-worn path
Memories come unbidden, choking
Welling tears in my eyes

I have come here tonight
In search of a promise
Time races by, blurring,
Alone, it fades even faster

Many a time there had been
Two shadows by the birch
Gentle souls of stirring whispers
Laughter melding in the stillness

Strange calmness of death
In its silence, this broken spirit
Sorrowing anguish of no end
Days of wanderless living

I have come here tonight
Searching for that promise
Tattered remnants of my being
Clutching at dwindling hope

Cool air brushes upon
My cheek, so tender was that caress
That fleeting night of long ago
Your love borne by the breeze

My heart brims with joy
The wind blowing more strongly
Streaks of dampness lie unmoving
Quieting the raging storm

I was loved and that
I'd always be
This the promise that I'd found
Love for all eternity and beyond.

Traffic

Everyday I lose myself
In the din of traffic life
Blaring horns and colored lights
Breaking this silence

Darting cars of painted rage
Open chaos on a stormy sea
The rush of air around my feet
Trembling heart-stopping breathlessness

People like scampering ants
Endless frenzy of fast-paced lives
The street for the moment
The ledge of our existence.

Crush

Everyday he drives by me
Sleek silver gray
Arrogant tilt, masses of coffee brown
Windblown carelessly

Cease this beating
Of a young heart driven
Sidelong glance of downcast eyes
Blooming cheeks in defiance

Beset by this strange shivering
Incoherent words tumbling
In a rush; fingers like
Flying needles, ever faster

Everything comes to a standstill
So still; gasping breath suspended
Always as he passes by
Coffee brown and sleek silver gray.

The Broken-Hearted

Gloom hangs in gray mists
Burdening souls of grief
Sunken eyes of tearless pools

Shroud of silence lays upon
Velvet black on whimpered cries
The barrenness of a withered heart

Shadows of deepest sorrow cling
Nights of quiet anguish
This life, a seeming nothingness.

Beloved Grandmother

There is the hint of a
Smile on the youthful face
A mystery of whispered charms
This, the face of the cameo lady.

Black demure eyes so concealing
A nature given to laughter
Pale features effortlessly reveal
A loving and generous heart.

A life touched with pain
Fate has not always been kind
She must have wavered, but
In the end, steadfast she remained.

Of her gentle and humble ways
I can speak kindly of;
Of her patient sufferings and comforting presence
I do well to remember by.

The smile plays on her lips
Subtle mystery of whispered charms
This, the face of the cameo lady
The face of my grandmother.

Washings

Washings on the open field
Underneath the great blue sky
Lemon scent a swirling mist
Stirring memories of another time

Grandmother with eyes so kind
Wrinkled hands and gentle touch
From where the water flows
Frothing bubbles so brightly gay

Scrub, wash, and soak them good
Many a time she'd say to me
So much a measure of a man
Washings do always tell

Scented sheets caress my face
Swirling me in their embrace
Grandmother laughed in joyous glee
Around them we danced that day

Little Anne will soon be six
Time for the lemon-scented mist
Because so much a measure of a man
Washings do always tell.

Coming Home

The craggy hillsides stand
Strong against the pounding surf
I have stood here once before

The wind blows none too gently
Whipping through my hair
Stinging my eyes with tears

The grass sighs beneath my feet
The heather blushing so
What tranquility, what isolation

I hear the song of the sea
Whisper soft voices on the breeze
Rousing a tide of emotion

This, the land of my birth
All around me, echoes of my past
I have come home to the moors.

The Best Time Of The Year

Snowflakes falling on the snow
Pure, white, ever so silent
Silver bells so merrily jingle
Happiness, laughter all here tonight.

The Christmas door opens and closes
Crackling fire on popping corn
Mistletoe and glistening balls
What excitement, this night of nights!

Every turn of the street
Merry Christmas! It's old Saint Nick
Come to journey on his reindeer sleigh
Ho, ho, ho! This season's cheers!

Shop windows quivering with frost
Naughty Jack Frost has come to play
Festive presents and pine-scented cones
'Tis Christmas, that time of year.

The Ritual

Small woman with teapot
Tiny feet shuffling on floor
Clatter of teacups loud
Ringing in my ears.

Small, piercing eyes stare
Words her mouth move
Hot liquid from the spout
Steaming wisps floating above.

Wrinkled hands clasped together
Sunlight on the glittering jade
Sweet incense in the air
Old portraits on the wall.

Tiny flame from a match
Joss sticks gathered together
Iron-grey head bows once
Twice, thrice, ever so respectful.

Beloved Gods and Ancestors
We honor you today
This feast we prepare
Invite your presence, stay.

Rustling of silk dress
Small woman, my grandmother
Walk away on noiseless feet
The ritual is complete.

A Chinese Daughter's Path

Sweet song of the nightingale
Bursts forth loudly in joy, freedom.
Pain in my heart, anguish
Today I leave my family
This is my destiny, tradition dictates.

Black hair perfectly swept up
Status of a married woman.
Hot tears scald my cheeks
Mother's heirlooms on my neck, arms
Like shackles, unyielding.

Fine rice powder on face so smooth
Red lips utter no words, trembling.
Gold and red silk, happiness
Phoenix and Dragon, prosperity
Must be happy, a good match.

Nothing is of my will;
As a daughter, this is my way.
Obedience, Humility, Respect of Elders
My duties are bound to my destiny
My heart, a stone in my chest.

The wedding party has arrived
Mother enters my room
Love in marriage very rare
More sons, more joy
Fewer daughters, fewer troubles.

I am led away from my room;
The house, perhaps forever.
No looking backwards, a new life
Old ties, everything must be forgotten
Bring honor to my family.

My feet shuffle noiselessly, following always
As it should be with my husband.
Meek and biddable wife most desirable
Matters of the heart no concern
Suffering in silence most sensible.

Great gods and honored ancestors
Give me strength to walk this path
Ease the burden of a leaden heart
Bless me now on my way
For my daughter shall walk here someday.

Charmed

(inspired by the television series Charmed)

On that rainy day you came
On board a taxi with no name
In grandma's house you came to stay
The city had driven you away

Playing with the board you wrought
Ancient powers we never sought
Beam of light falling free
Gifting us dear sisters three

Flying objects, power of mind
Prue is never far behind
Freezing everything to a still
Piper bends time to her will

Phoebe can with a touch of hand
Watch past and future unfold as planned
In this manor the charmed ones dwell
Nothing ordinary about the Halliwells

Warlocks and demons we must fight
Protecting the innocents from evil's plight
The Book of Shadows always by
Reminding us never to doubt why

For personal gain remember to keep
Or consequences we shall reap

How changed our lives have been
Only time will tell what all these mean

We have come as was foretold
The Warren legacy ours to hold
For in this manor, the charmed ones dwell
Prue, Piper, and Phoebe Halliwell.

Life On A Photograph

The faded photograph sits on my desk
Glinting rays of sun bouncing off
Its worn and ragged edges
The touch of a caressing hand
Lingering on the smiling faces.

The smiles of youthful hopes
Joyous anticipation of golden
Horizons; aglow with the
Promise of life to be lived
Walking along life's pathway.

Sorrow would darken some days
Leaden clouds of melancholy
Pain and sadness marring
Such wounds do slowly heal
Time's passage a soothing balm.

Wisdom like trickles of sand
Surer and wiser with age
Lightened laughter and purest joy
Brilliance never dimming
Beacons on the blackest nights.

Love always for the sharing
Hopes and promises all to
Be cherished; dreams in the
Waiting, friendship warming the heart.

The photograph sits on my desk
Glinting rays bouncing off the gleaming surface
Smiles and creases on the faces
The touch of a caressing hand
Promise of a life well-lived.

In The Days Of My Youth

In the days of my youth
I knew of Love
Unconditionally; hushed whispers
And cherished thoughts, of ardent
Embraces in the gleam of twilight.

In the days of my youth
I knew of Care
A soothing hand; healing words,
Cool lips on a burning brow
Comfort in the gloom of desolation.

In the days of my youth
I knew of Friendship;
Through stormy gales and peaceful days,
Of talks and musings aplenty
A constant cup of piping tea.

In the days of my youth
I knew of Laughter
Unbridled; unconcealed in its turn
A most soothing balm for the
Weary soul.

In the days of my youth
I knew of Happiness;
Deep-seated and true
All-encompassing
In its reach.

In the days of my youth
I knew of Peace
Tranquility; its shroud over me
Long moments of solitude
And quiet harmony.

And now, way past the flush of youth
Love, Care, Friendship, Laughter
Happiness and Peace I have known
And always will keep at
My side, forever.

My Heart, My Love

I look at you in peaceful slumber
And I wonder if you know
Just how much I love you
And how much you mean to me

The way moonlight touches your hair
Silvery white on deepest black

The way you say my name
Hushed velvet on satin waves

Your arms, strong yet gentle
Moorings on stormy gales

Your voice, speaking of love
And concern, tender huskiness

Your footprints beside me all the way
Shielding, protecting

Your eyes, eloquently a myriad
Of cherishing, caring, and laughing

Your heart, its steady beating
In tune to my joyous cadence

I look at you in peaceful slumber
And I know that you know
Just how much I love you
And how much you mean to me.

May The Blessing Of God Be Upon You

A young and most winsome bride
Of roses blooming in her cheeks
Of tender and caring hands
Of loving with purest heart

A dashing and handsome groom
Of stalwart strength and comfort
Lifelong devotion to a true love
An undying pledge

Passion to sweeten many a
Night; sweet kisses and
Whispered murmurs amidst
Darkened embers

Love for the sharing and giving
Burning fiercely
Weathering life's storms and
Fickle winds

Hope always to be had
Of things yet to come
For tomorrow's uncertainties
Standing strongly together

Joy, lasting and enduring
Coming into full circle
Hope for this new start
Be blessed till the end.

The Wishing Well

Deep in the shadowy glen
Time cannot tell when
Stands a wishing well of wrought stone
Perhaps by angel's wings it was borne.

The sparkling waters so crystal clear
Once mirroring a reflection of love so dear
Its smoothened walls of mossy green
Telling of what cannot be seen.

A sweet familiar strain
The shimmering echoes of deep refrain
Of fragrant nights and young a swain
Tenderly these moments remain.

Where once a maiden's thoughts must dwell
Hoping in the wishing well
For a knight to arrive
Whisk her off to be his cherished bride.

A place for promises to keep
On ancient vows the lovers sleep
Placid the waters upon it swirl
Dancing to a long-forgotten twirl.

Beneath the rose arbor it stays
True love always finds a way
Its solitary quest not fading by
Endlessly under the bluest sky.

Cinderella

(inspired from the fairytale collection of Charles Perrault and the Grimm Brothers)

Once and far away in a manor
Lived a wealthy man and his
Beautiful, kind-hearted daughter

She had grown up without a mother
And so hoping to ease her plight
The father paid court and married another

But this joyous time was brief
The father was soon dearly departed
The little girl alone in her grief

With her cruel and wicked ways
The stepmother banished her to
Sweep cinders and the hearth to stay

With the girl unrightfully disowned
She and her daughters set about
Making her whereabouts unknown

How quickly the years had passed
With all her work, Cinderella
Had no time to dwell on her past

Growing more beautiful by the day
Unchanged in sweetness and temperament
In her heart, dreams and wishes lay

One morn, quite a stir there be in the house
The geese flapped with excitement, the
Old horse, too, down to the tiny mouse

The prince was having a ball
And maidens from the kingdom
Were to come, one and all

What delight! Oh what glee!
For the lady he chooses
His coveted bride she shall be

Her looks so unkempt
Filthy and tattered rags clinging
How Cinderella's wounded heart wept

Suddenly a glimmer of light
Sparkling beams of magical dust
Lit the dark of night

"Hush, don't cry my child,"
Her fairy godmother said
"In this carriage you shall ride."

A well-sprung coach of such class
And on her tiny feet
Exquisite slippers of finest glass

A gown of spangled silk and lace
Cinderella could only admire
This dress, she must wear with grace

Pay these words with heed
Be home tonight by twelve
For undone shall come this deed

She was a magnificent sight at the ball
Everyone stopped and stared
No one recognized her at all

She had roused his heart
And as he danced with her longer
He could not bear for them to part

The clock had struck by then
Cinderella hurriedly broke away
Would ever they meet again

Only a glass slipper he found
Desperate were his efforts
Her presence lingering all around

A proclamation he duly signed
The lady who fits the slipper
In marriage he would bind

Her stepsisters tried to fit their feet
With all their might, but failed,
Inside the slipper so slight

It broke under duress
Leaving the Grand Duke trembling
And stuttering with stress

Whereupon Cinderella took out the other
All gasped to see, disbelieving,
The dazzling piece is none other

The prince, he took her to marry
After so long a time searching
Why should he still tarry?

Happily ever after this tale ends
For Cinderella and her prince
Their love was truly heaven-sent.

The Romanovs

The Romanovs were Imperial Russia's
Ruling royal family
And they remained so
Until the early years of the 20th century.

Tsar Nicholas was to the manor born
And though he liked it not
He was heir to the throne
In life that was his lot.

It was the Princess Alexandra who won his heart
Of all the princesses he could have had
And his father prepared a lavish nuptial feast
Of his son's choice he was glad.

Of their early married life
The years were blissful
Four lovely daughters, and at last a son
They had so much to be thankful.

Olga, Tatiana, Maria, and Anastasia
And Nicholas's heir, Alexis,
To be soon marred by tragedy
Who would have thought a Fate as theirs could exist?

The old tsar suddenly died
And Nicholas was thrust into the glare.
The people's expectations, his weighty duties and obligations
All conspired to strip him bare.

For Nicholas was a gentle man
More suited to stay behind the scene.
He would have gladly yielded his throne
At his happiest he would have been.

His people were restless
Driven by poverty and hunger.
The clamors and cries for revolution and revolt
Posing an imminent danger.

They felt that their Tsar
Had been derelict in his duty
Concerning himself with interests of opulence
And objects that caught his fancy.

But Nicholas was shielded from all these
By his advisers' own ambitions
Protecting the King from reality
Rejecting change in the name of tradition.

So dependent had the tsarina on Rasputin become,
The self-appointed healer of her son's affliction
In court matters did he interfere
Tainting his majesties' decisions.

His people all felt at a loss
With the Bolsheviks, they toppled the monarchy
Leaving in its stead
Tattered remnants of a once-powerful royalty.

The Tsar and his family
Left a captive in their own country
In his beloved Alix's arms

He found steadfast love and loyalty.

On a cold winter's day
They were herded unceremoniously into the basement room.
The sounds of gunfire and the
Bloodstained walls permeated the eerie gloom.

Such a tragic fate to have suffered
Their lives quickly snuffed out.
One can only wonder
What their last thoughts were about.

In the hearts of those whom they have touched
The scarred wound silently grieves
For they who have died
Vanishing like the snow upon the eaves.

The Ballad Of Lord Geoffrey And Margaret

In the darkest hour of night
The ancients, with wistful eyes, will say
Soft whisperings echo in the glen
Shadows with arms entwined in loving embrace
The grass unbent beneath their feet.

Lord Geoffrey was to the riches born
His handsome looks and easy charm
Belying a kind-hearted and generous nature;
Though wealth and power he had,
His people loved him for his heart.

Margaret, for that was her name,
Was the village merchant's daughter
Of blackest hair and fairest skin;
Beauty to rival the rose; purity
Unsullied by a touch of sin.

Geoffrey loved her truly
And she in turn with him
Many secret nights in the glen
They had vowed their love and devotion;
The gleaming moon in mute witness.

How filled with ire the father
Curses and threats upon his son,
But Geoffrey remained unmoved
Only more resolute he grew
Till his father lost the cause.

How gladdened he was to hear
Of his father's acceptance
And with haste he sought
Margaret; she
Rejoicing at the joyous news.

But all was not what it seemed
For the elder had a deceitful heart.
She would never be his bride,
Not a drop of her blood
Would ever taint their name.

And so he commanded his son
On some pretended quest;
This he had to do before
Living in wedded bliss.
With no misgivings, Geoffrey bade farewell.

Many days flew past.
Margaret, diligent on her bridal finery
Overseeing the preparations
For her coming nuptial day,
Thoughts always resting on her beloved.

When suddenly news broke upon them
Lord Geoffrey was dead.
He had been attacked by bandits

And was slain in battle.
Weeping carried on the passing breeze.

Margaret was faint with grief.
The hands which had lovingly sewn her gown
Now hung limp.
She moved trance-like to the one
Place where they had been happiest.

The solitary figure in the glen
Never to see sunrise upon
His beloved face; fated to spend her days
In endless wandering
And unceasing pain.

If not in life then in death
They shall be together.
She willingly let life ebb from
Her; falling to sleep never
To awaken again.

Unaware of his father's treachery
Geoffrey came upon the throng.
White-faced villagers mourning his demise;
The crescendo of babbled voices
Filling him with dread.

 Lying soft upon the grass
Her beauty unmarred by death;
The loving eyes that had once
Caressed him; the laughter that
Had roused his heart, stilled.

He had lain beside her
She in his clasped embrace
As it always had been.
His blood a crimson trail
Stark against her fairest skin.

And so the ancients say
That in the darkest hour of night
Lord Geoffrey and Margaret walk the glen
Their love undimmed by time
Untouched by Death.

To Dare A Quiet Heart: For Dean And Jo

(inspired by the television series, Supernatural)

It was never my intention
To dare a quiet heart

A heart that had too much of a past
You were sure nobody could ever grasp

I sensed it the moment you came in
The feeling of rightness that came from within

Of all the men I've met and seen
You were someone I never dared to dream

And then you walked in the door
And my young heart beat once more

I am never so subtle
Perhaps wanting too much, never too little

You treat me offhand, like a little sister
But I have never looked at you as my brother

I know you think this is just an infatuation
Between a man and a woman, the problem of this situation

But I like, perhaps, even love you
Is it so hard to believe it might be true?

Because of my youth, don't set me aside
If you will just let me, I am in for the long ride

I know and understand more than you do
The dangers that loving someone might put them through

Although you have never said it, you cannot bear another loss
You brace your heart, but still the fear comes across

Let it not impede what you might feel for me
If there is something, can you not let it be?

I, too, have known the pain of loss
Surely a burden shared by two will lighten the cross

I have strength and courage far beyond my years
More than any other, I know your fears

I, too, have demons that plague me in the night
Unanswered questions and tortured musings never set to right

It tears me in two; in liking, even loving you
Am I betraying my father's memory, too?

There must be something to explain the way it happened
Surely it could not just be how it ended

And so you are now far away from me
Yet despite the anger and the hurt; it is still you I wish to see

At night, I always pray for the safety of your return
Fervent hope inside me still burns

That perhaps you might begin to feel something for me
If not love, then something close to it, let it be

After all, it never was my intention
To dare a quiet heart

But now that I did
Perhaps it is time that we had a start.

Heartland Song

The rocker sits silent facing the quiet land
Its worn surface touched by a wrinkled hand

I slowly slide into the seat
My pulse echoing with a thudding beat

I raise the cup of coffee to my lips
Drinking of the aromatic brew in a long-drawn sip

The sun has begun to settle in the west
Soon you will be beside me, the time I like best

How long ago was it when upon this porch we stood
Imbued with a newlywed's joyous mood

We gazed out as one upon the vast and open land
As we start the long road, hand in hand

You toiled the fields and worked the land
Morning and night like the drifting sand

Our children who came by birth
Blessings upon this sweet earth

Our lives have not been without its share of pain
But tenfold the happiness we have gained

I look at us all seated by the hearth
And I know that all our sacrifices have been worth

Our love has stayed strong and true
Not once have you given me cause to rue

It has been years since that day
And still my heart is here to stay

In this land and in your hand
Faithfully as the glimmering golden band

Now you climb the steps and sit beside me
As we look out beyond the canopy of trees

I feel the touch of your lips against my hair
Its very tenderness leaving my soul bare

The caress of your hand a gentle sweep
Against my lined and weathered cheek

I see my love echoed in your eyes
It is the binding cord that ties

My heart, my land I see
All that I had ever dreamed to be.

In Ode To Emily Elizabeth Dickinson

Perhaps on the night she was born
The night itself was lonely and forlorn

The stars must have been gleaming dully in the sky
When the infant girl gave her first cry

Her destiny must have been charted then
Great things to come from her though no one could comprehend

She grew up in a distinguished family
Among academicians and statesmen well-known in the community

Sent off to the finest schools
At a time when gender and not equality was the rule

She came home to Amherst
Closeting herself inside her room, thoughts did she nurse

Shy, gentle, and withdrawn
She seemed lost in a world of her own

She became a recluse by choice
But to her feelings and emotions she gave a voice

Writing about love, immortality, and things she did know
The seated figure touched by the lamp's glow

She walked the gardens in the dusky twilight
As seen by those in the streets out of her sight

What went on behind her shadowed eyes
A great loneliness she could not disguise

Perhaps pining for an unrequited love
Sent on prayer's swift wings to above

Piece by hundred piece she wrote
Sheaves of parchment flooding her like an endless moat

And when she felt that her life was at the end
She must have looked beyond the bend

Death in his carriage soon came driving by
She closed her eyes with a peaceful sigh

'Twas only years after her death
The scope of her works and its depth

Praises heaped upon her by the world
Accolades by the dozen lay unfurled

She who had written,
"Who are you? Me, I am nobody."
Destined to become
One of the greatest poets of the nineteenth century.

The Haunt Of The Wolfman

When the night wind blows in from the north
With it they say the Wolfman comes forth

The people hammer the windows and pace the floor
Wooden crosses in abundance shielding the door

A nameless fear sends chills down their spine
The flickering candles casting long shadows behind

Even the babe in the cradle lies all hushed
The air's eerie stillness dark and untouched

The people huddle deeper within their cowls
Their faces raised in dread at the blood-curdling howl

Onto their knees they sink and begin to pray
For morning light to drive the devil's beast away

Fervent Pater Nosters and Ave Marias from of age
Inciting the creature to a bloodthirsty rage

Into the village it rushes in leaps and bounds
The monstrous paws striking the earth, a heathen sound

Its yellow eyes alight in fiendish glee
Upon this malevolent sight all must flee

Its claws like a hundred knives cut through the air
Tearing flesh, leaving no bone bare

The ivory fangs that cut and rip
Crimson trails on the ground from where it drips

No man or beast has ever been spared in its rampage
In its wake only sorrow and bloodied carnage

The village can only suffer in silence
Praying for it to end, their only penance

For deep in their hearts they nurse
The ugly secret of this seemingly endless curse

'Twas over a hundred years ago
When this village was just formed so

Everywhere contentment and peace could be found
Familial love and joy did abound

But a sudden ill upon them soon struck
Livestock and people did it destruct

Sordid tales of unproven claims were soon brewed
Twisting the elders' minds with words often misconstrued

Driven by the clamor of the town gathering
The elders could do naught but join in the accusing

The old woman who had but done no wrong
Except that 'twas her life which would appease the throng

They screamed for her blood to be spilt
Insinuations that she was a witch drove their emotions to the hilt

Sentenced to die, to burn at the stake
Against their rabid outpouring the decision she could not unmake

Stones and sticks they did throw and taunt
This innocent woman, by her death she would haunt

The fiery flames licked her as the morning dawned
Before she was gripped by death, she called on Satan's spawn

From the depths of hell she summoned the hellish beast
To avenge her wrongful death till she bid it cease

This curse she heaped upon their heads
From her vengeful countenance, in terror they fled

And it was soon after her death
That this evil crept upon them with stealth

And so it has been for a hundred years
The village numbed and silenced by its fear

Always when the night wind blows in from the north
The Wolfman it brings forth

To purge the village of its sin
If only to see repentance upon their mien.

Remember Me

Remember me
As one who loved you
Hushed as the whispers of the night

Remember me
As one who loved you
In the stirred longings of your embrace

Remember me
As one who loved you
In my heart, your yearnings are silenced

Remember me
As one who loved you
When the moon rose upon the dying morn

Remember me
As one who loved you
Till the seas have stilled their cries

Remember me
As one who loved you
When but Death has made its presence felt.

Reflections On A Rainy Day

This rainy and stormy weather
Prevents us from being together

The clouds gather in gray and somber gloom
Loneliness making my heart its room

I think back to the sunny days
When we were together everyday

The familiar pathways we walked on
Conversations drifting like a lingering song

The scent of honeysuckle hung in the air
The black-eyed susans with their shy stare

Our hands clasped together
Our heads nestled against each other

Now I sit beneath the dark leaden sky
Wondering how time could still drift by

Passing me on dragging feet
Making me ache to weep

I fervently hope for this rain to pass
Bringing to my heart joyous seasons to last.

My Infatuation: A Teenage Girl's Point Of View

I see him everyday
The boy I like
I try not to look at him
Silently hoping he'd glance my way.

We meet in class
And as I quickly move to take my seat
I slip and fall against him
The start of the day, and already I feel like an ass.

He catches my hand
Helps me with my books
I quickly mumbled my thanks
Vaguely pronounced words he'd never understand.

He looks at me strangely
"Are you all right?" he asks
I nodded, unable to breathe
Something I was always unable to do, until lately.

I could not concentrate on History
My pen doodling on blank, white sheets

Wishing the French revolution to perdition
And I could begin my own story.

It's strange, this thing called infatuation
Suddenly I like him
But I'm not sure how he feels about me
Sure! A one-sided attraction.

I start worrying over much everything
My hair, my school uniform,
The way I act and speak in class
Even the littlest thing amounts to something!

I have silly smiles on my face
Finding myself awkwardly self-conscious
And feeling most unnatural and a klutz
I wish to be out of this phase.

I find myself mooning over him
Watching sappy old movies and
Imagining myself in every love song
How foolish this all seems.

This is not me
How changed I am from before
Well, I guess when one gets twitterpated
This is the way it's supposed to be.

The onset of puberty
My Science teacher would say
If my parents did not undergo this torture
I wouldn't be here today.

Finally, class has ended for the day
I close my books and sneak a glance
Only to find him with a smile
Making me blush as I make my way.

"Alexandra, I'll see you around."
He knew my name!
I silently squealed, his scent
And nearness surround.

I walked to the door on wings
I knew I could have flown if I wanted to
Anything was possible
I could do undreamed-of things.

I fairly skipped my way
My thoughts of him and me
Really, sometimes teenage infatuation
Can make your day.

Once Upon A Tranquil Moor

Tranquility shrouds the moors
At night
The shimmering stars a shadow
On it blight

The desolate grass do part
To make a way
The passing mournful wind
Do the gentle bracken sway

On a star-filled eve
So long ago
Scarlet blood and silver tears
Did silently flow

The night spoke of a bonny lass
With raven-black hair
And looks to rival the sun
She was beauteous fair

The laird of the clan loved her so
Her presence was bliss
Of her loving and caring ways
Her heart was truly his

The joyful news that she
Was to bear a child
Cast a glimmer of hope
On dread and anguish he could not hide

He must go and
Ride at first light
Together with his king
The pillaging renegades they would fight

With bitter tears and a lasting kiss
Did they part in sorrow
Hearts shaken in their very depths
Would ever they meet on the morrow

The battle was fought
For long and hard
Near its end, the laird was felled
By an arrow which pierced his guard

Of this tragedy, his lady knew of none
Save for the sudden chilling emptiness
When on their bed
She sought to find her rest

The pain was soon upon her, so quick
The midwives beside her wept
Taking its toll on her body
Her frail life so suddenly swept

Born too soon before his time
The infant uttered not a cry
Cradled within her bosom
Amidst the heather they slept by

But for this single night of every year
When tranquility shrouds the moors
And the stars' dim light
On it pours

The desolate grass do part
To make a way
Glistening moonlight on the path
Suddenly bright as day

Husky laughter and an infant's
Cry of sweet refrain
Where true love abides
Death's hand is always in vain.

Of Lovers' Night

The day has come to an end
Darkening shadows slowly descend

Black shall soon be the color of night
The silvery moon our only light

The cold night wind will soon caress
A fragrant, wayward tress

My eyes ache to see
The beloved form beneath the oak tree

I long to hear the poignant strain
Like the dying melody of a song's refrain

To be swept in your tender embrace
To see the look of love upon your face

To have your lips softly speak my name
These wondrous nights of love unwaned

I fly to you on feet so light
Upon the scented grass to take flight

For the day has been too long
To you and the night I have always belonged

Wait! Oh, do wait! For your love is here
Enfold me then and keep me forever near.

Wildflowers In The Field

We met on the wildflower field
When Summer brought forth its yearly yield

I was barefooted, my feet touching the dusty ground
The scent of the wildflowers redolent all around

You stretched out your hand, tanned and strong
Smooth with nary a rough patch, fingers lean and long

We spent the afternoon walking with the sun
Your nearness making my heart beat a staccato run

Your whispered words hung in the air
And my heart to you I openly bared

Our promises mingling sweet and tender
Two souls beating as one forever

Summer will slip away for Autumn's turn
But my love, to you, I'll always return

On the train I bade you goodbye
All alone I breathed a forlorn sigh

I raised my hand against the sun to shield
And saw the wildflowers dancing in the field

Not a sound I heard, not a word to say
And still the flowers were bright and gay

I hoped for the remembrance of a glance, a smile
So far away from you, so many miles

Time has passed and there has been no post
My heart has been given a sweet repose

How wrenching the pain, it seems
Gripped by a vise, unseen

The torment gives me no peace
I rush into the field seeking surcease

The wildflowers sway in the field
Against the sun's rays their petals wield

How foolish had been this heart
To ever believe I could be a part

The wildflowers had known all along
His love had never been that strong

I look at them and bow my head
Hiding from their prying eyes, this wound freshly bled

I spend the afternoon dancing in the sun
Tears unchecked down my cheeks in a run

While the wildflowers stand bright against the field
Offering to the sky their bountiful yield.

The Lost Children Of Hamelin

(inspired from the fairy tale collection of the Grimm Brothers)

Over the hill and beyond the mountain
Stands a lonely, forgotten village
Footsteps do not break the stillness
Nor water flows from the silent fountain

Empty space from beyond the door
Cobwebs hang from ancient beams
A child's long-forgotten wooden toy
Lay mute upon the dusty floor

And yet you feel in the very wind
Its cold, biting deep
Unknown things that our
Mortal eyes cannot have seen

The village was once alive with life
Teeming with people
And all commonplace emotions
Love, Care, Greed, and Strife

Children filled the cobblestone streets
Their shrieks and laughter
A cacophony of sound
Spiraling into the midday heat

All this shattered by a serious malady
Rats, many numbers of them
Swarming the kitchens, the houses
And along the many alleys

The mayor could only shake his head
How could he hope to find
The answers to his besieged village
He sought other means instead

A stranger strolled into town
With his jaunty hat and musical pipe
They whispered behind his back
Furrowed foreheads in a frown

So it was that he struck a deal
A fee for his services
And as he played upon his pipe
Excited cries and eager squeals

For the rats were wont to follow him
Scurrying, hurrying, following the strange
Hypnotic melody all the way to the river
Jumping in, never again to be seen

When the task was done, the piper asked for his pay
But the mayor and his people
Laughed and turned against their word
Rigid with anger, the Piper walked away

That night, when all were asleep
The Piper began to play his pipe
All the children rose out of bed
Their parents unknowing, sleeping deep

How the children ran and laughed with glee
Following the yellow-dressed man in the jaunty cap
Over the hill and into the mountain
It closed and there was no trace left to see

With morning came the reality
All their children were gone
And no matter where they searched
Defeat in their eyes, and in their voices a finality

Because of their foul deed
Suffer they should their loss
In exchange for a sack of coins
How high was the price indeed

Nothing was ever found of them
Nor of the strange, foreign man
It was as if events conspired to
Make them unable to comprehend

But some folks say that if you listen closely by
You can hear the shrieks and laughter of children at play
And above the din, the Piper's melody
Floating by like a distant sigh.

Love-forsaken Bride

When the night itself is so still
In the great manse, the wind blows its eerie chill

Unlit candles on lonely sconces flicker with life
Casting dancing shadows on the long-abandoned fife

Haunting strains of a forgotten melody
Enveloped in graying mists of melancholy

There, there! Look upon the bare stair
Silent, satin-shod feet on rugs so threadbare

The hand so pale, touching upon the rusted rail
So soft, so soft the keening wail

Hear not, hear not the mournful, agonizing sound
A tortured soul to this earth she's bound

Crumpled satin and yellowed lace as she makes her way
The figure, untouched by time's decay

The eyes shadowed by the spidery veil
Startling blue as a ship upon the sea had sailed

Gardenia-fragrant tresses of ebony twilight
Never has a tragic figure been a lovelier sight

And yet one feels not a tinge of fear
Instead, pervading sadness from the figure so near

Slowly she comes to a still in the great hall
The wilted bouquet halting the petals' fall

Standing by, waiting to pledge her troth
To the gallant, handsome knight, her betrothed

Unknowing that his life had been snatched by Death's hand
Never to be his wife; upon her finger, never to wear the wedding band

So it has been for years and years
The lamented figure in her agony and endless tears

She, spending eternity alone in her satin and lace
Her life never to be touched by love's grace.

If Autumn Shall Linger

If Autumn shall linger
Its demise I certainly will not hinder

She will mark the leaves maple-brown and amber
And still her passing, I shall not hinder

The trees with their souls barren and stark
With Autumn, the onset of eternal dark

How still is Life and how long are the nights
The increasing shadows upon this world a blight

The early, muted sounds of twilight
To chase the last, stubborn rays of daylight

Brittle, dying leaves a fine carpeting upon the forest floor
A stately welcome just outside Winter's door

I still wish that Autumn would linger
Of the dying warm rays, she is the bringer

With her passing shall come Winter in her imperial chill
Her coming, for me, only bodes ill

I cannot bear to see Autumn in her demise
Her death-dance a pained reflection in my eyes

If the seasons have to pass like a litany of prayers
I wish Autumn would linger on forever.

The Legend Of The Stone-Cast Prince

The legend of the bold and valiant prince
How long has it been since

Was there ever more a truer and tragic tale
As the villagers were wont to tell over a tankard of ale

To any who would come to listen
While the dewdrops hanging on the trembling leaf glisten

Hundreds of years it was before we were ever born
When pledges of fealty upon the lords were sworn

Where before this barren land stands, a kingdom once stood
Fortune was benevolent and the land was good

The harvests were always a-plenty
Baskets of bread and goblets never running empty

But unto this blessed time a shadow soon cast
A darkening menace held them in its clasp

Strange beasts tore through the night
Ravaging, tearing everything in sight

Huge creatures with blood-red eyes and rapier claws
Poisoned drool dripping from cavernous maws

Death and carnage to every creature they brought
The valiance of the men counted for naught

The once golden fields bright with blood
Endless torrent of tears like a sweeping flood

The king could only moan in despair
All of his men dying, none would be left to spare

In desperation, he sent his messengers far and wide
To the beast-slayer, his daughter to give as his bride

Many came in answer to his summons
For it was heard that the daughter's looks were most uncommon

Her beauty so great, found none to compare
Staring into her eyes, they were forever ensnared

Many came to join the fight
But none ever returned at first light

Even the king had begun to lose hope
His shaking hands, increasingly for drink began to grope

When the kingdom's end seemed but near
A last challenger did appear

Even now when much time has passed, they say that he was a sight to behold
Magnificent in stature, his armor glistening like gold

His services he offered to the king
This prince from nowhere whom nobody knew a thing

But they saw by the flint in his eye
He was to be their deliverer; no longer would they cry

With his broadsword and mace in hand
He soon laid to rest the beasts that were the scourge of the land

The long, white fangs sinking into the soil
The poisoned fumes mingling with the peasants' toil

The land and people rejoiced once more
Surely with him as their next king, no more grief to come upon them like before

But no one had thought to pay the princess any heed
Her frigid heart did not thaw at this bold deed

Indeed, she planned a way to let death do them part
For to another had she given her heart

It was in the stillness of the night
She and her father's conjurer did well plan out of sight

By his craft, he had called the beasts
Upon this hapless kingdom's flesh to feast

Until the old king would yield his throne
And he would wield power all his own

But these plans had been dashed to the wind
By the stranger who had come from parts unseen

So they sought to flee on her wedding day
Before the sun rose, they would be far away

But the prince, sensing something was amiss
Rode after them in the graying mists

Black magic tore through his flesh and bone
Everywhere they touched, turning him to stone

The boat carrying the wicked pair sank on the first wave
Sweeping them deep into an endless grave

But he who had rescued the kingdom, remained locked in stone
Through all this time he has been mourned

A prince with no greater sin than to have loved
A woman unworthy of life from above

He shall stay cast in stone
Until she who loves him truly shall be born

Only then shall her tears break the spell
Bringing him to life; making true the prophecy many have come to tell

So the prince, with his sightless eyes is waiting still
For the promise of love to be fulfilled.

To A Girl Of Fifteen

Today, you are just turned fifteen
And I find myself searching for words
To fit in this little poem's seams

So much has changed these days
From both our points of view
We are likely to say

But still some things remain the same
As constant and as certain
As the sunrise when it came

Imbue your life with Love
The greatest of all virtues
Truly, a gift from heaven above

Seek for Friendship that is true
One that will stand the stormy gales
And fill your days with lovely hues

Do keep your loved ones always near
Do not wait for such a time as they are gone
To tell them they are dear

Be sure to have a wealth of Laughter and Smiles
A bit of cheer, a dash of yellow sunshine
They make life's darker moments worthwhile

Do possess a heart for Compassion and Understanding
In them, your soul will find itself gentled
And you will find meaning in living

Patience to help you know
And Courage to stouten yourself
When the winds in their fury blow

Faith to be a candle in the dark
Always a spark of Hope
When sometimes all turns bleak and stark

Sorrow, Pain, and Loneliness will not last
As sure as change will come about
These things will always pass

Do dream your dreams
But do not be disheartened
When it's not what it seems

Caution then to let yourself fly not too high
There is nothing so frustrating
As wanting a piece of unattainable sky

Lean on your strengths and accept your flaws
Our strengths can better us and our
Flaws, in humility, can help us grow

Do not be so harsh when you fail
And remember that it is sometimes at life's lowest ebb
That the human spirit prevails

Pray not for overconfidence; for the brashness of the young
Be open to the words of others, you have yet unheard-of
Songs waiting to be sung

Hurry not with words of hurt and thoughts of anger
Long after the scorching flames have died
The embers of hurt will linger

Do have time to be merry, too
After all, everything is not just
Colored gray and blue

Celebrate each day and live
Fill it with wonder and you will
Be amazed at what life has to give

Find Joy in the simplest of things
There is to be found in most everything
A little of life's blessings

There is still so much left unsaid
So much for you to learn
But those, I will let Life guide you instead

Fifteen is a new beginning
Walk Life, Live in it, Journey through it
And at its end, may you find your own sweet ending.

Life In A Coffee Cup

To put my thoughts in a coffee cup
My thoughts one morning when the sun was not yet up and about

I absentmindedly put the kettle on to boil
My confused and frantic thoughts leaving me in turmoil

I wanted quiet, peaceful time to be alone
The comforting silence offered by a sleeping home

Assurance and Affirmation I was searching for
I felt I needed to learn more

I have at times felt overwhelmed by it all
Life itself leaving me feeling so small

How my hours in a day always seem lacking
And I end up trying to fit in everything

How instead of pacing myself to enjoy my life
I have to be an employee, a mother, and a wife

There had to be more, surely this wasn't just it
And so with coffee cup in hand, I thought to sit

I poured the water, steaming and clear
Shocked to see my reflection in it so near

Like Life on a blank sheet, life in a cup
As yet uncolored, untouched, as yet to start about

I spooned coffee--thick, dark, and bitter
Like grief, despair, anxiety, and hurt--times when things were not better

Sugar came next--pristine, clear, and sweet
Joy, hope, love, and peace--life's lovely treats

I found my thoughts clearing and startling
The growing realizations set my hand trembling

The creamer I now added to the swirling hues
The coffee was now complete and true

The cream to balance light and dark
The ensuing result--life never too black nor too stark

A little of everything, never too much of both
Gentle reminders to keep us afloat

Life is the bitter and the sweet; the happy and the sad
The hurt with the comfort; the good with the bad

Life gives us everything
And we find the answers within

How the blend of all those
Makes for a most aromatic brew, wafting across

And so on that quiet morn, before everyone was up and about
I looked down and saw Life in a coffee cup.

To Him Who Has My Love

My love, he comes at the beginning of day
With me, he has breathed forever to stay

His very presence has stilled my yearning
His very touch ceasing my trembling

The encroaching shadows he has banished far
No sorrow upon this face to mar

My heart rejoices in his cherishing
Leaps at his love, steadfast and lasting

His words of loveliness and joy
True, never a casual nor flirtatious ploy

His eyes of tender mirth and yet behold
A heart loyal and courageously bold

His love I hold against the buffeting winds
From things and future yet unseen

The promises he has given me
The passage of time has proved them be

I have chosen and loved him who is right
Ever so near, his love my guiding light

In him, I have found myself alive
These emotions, never false nor contrived

As on that day I took his hand
Man and wife, side by side we did stand.

Betrayal: A Friendship's End

What would you have me think of you?
My best friend once so true

Before we used to walk hand in hand
In the shadows of the trees we used to stand

Chatter and laughter filled our days
Together we chased our blues away

School and play were so much fun
Blowing dreams under the midday sun

I had thought that you were my forever friend
The only one until the very end

But it seems that things have about them a way
Change comes and nothing ever stays

A mask slipped upon your face
Your chilling distance left me no place

All alone and confused am I
And yet your silence no answer to the reason why

I try to search every memory
Was there ever a time when I needed to say I'm sorry?

So I unceasingly torment myself in the dark
Your dead eyes no light to spark

I quell my tears--my heart, its agonizing cries
The chasm between us you never realize

I long to reach, to touch, to plead
I am your friend, in word as well as in deed

And yet you choose not to bridge this space
Leaving me stranded in this empty place

If you will just let me in, tell me what's within
I am all hopes for us to begin

But please do not let me wait for so long
Even this stalwart heart is not that strong

I have withstood the pain too much
I can only hold until such

If this will go too long a breach
You might find me out of reach

So before regrets mark this friendship's end
My thoughts to you in this poem I'll send

And under the trees I shall stand
Waiting to hold you by the hand.

Sam And Jane: A Married Couple's Story

Sam and Jane had been set
On a blind date
And that was how they met

Sam was like a bean
With the bluest eyes
Tall and lean

Jane was like a reed
Slender and willowy
A great gel indeed!

After getting to know each other
They asked their parents' consent
To live as man and wife together

None could have been happier
Relatives and friends came to
Attend the wedding and make it merrier

And so it was love
A celebration made more special
With blessings from above

They started each and everyday
Jane to cook and bake
And Sam to work to make his way

The babies soon came
One, two, three
And life was never again the same

Jane who loved to cook
Became too tired to
Open the recipe book

So she set to ordering by phone
Fast-food dinners
Ready for Sam when he came home

Juicy burgers fit for a king
Fried chicken and crispy fries
Mayonnaise on the side for that zing!

At times chinese noodles in a pot
Crackled pork skin
So tasty and hot

Sam, too, had his faults
Buying cans of soda and beer
The caffeine giving that needed jolt

In the grocery he'd buy loads of chips
Cookies, candies, and sweets
And a whole lot of other dips

The greens vanished from their plates
Carrots and peas
Became the veggies they loved to hate

Fatty bacon and fire-roasted ham
Ice cream, pies, and cakes
On the table spread along with Spam

Ten years from the day they wed
They didn't bear a resemblance to
The couple in the pictures above their bed

Jane was now plump as a hen
From a size two
She had become a ten

Sam, too, had piled on the weight
With his rounded belly
He now looked like a figure eight

Here this little story ends be
Whether Sam and Jane did lose the weight
Dear readers, what do you see?

So, newlyweds do beware
Marriage can make you fat
And that's a fact you must be aware.

Danny Half-naked Saved My Week

(inspired from the character of Danny Messer in the television series, CSI NY)

It has been a horrid week
And to explain it all to you
Takes away so much of my breath
It renders me unable to speak

So to start from the top
I would have to say my life is so tragic
Parents attend PTAs, right
Can they not make the teachers stop?

I had three lab papers due
And when I switched on my PC
It chose that day to gasp, shudder
And then just turn cold and blue

Oh woe! Oh, gloomy academic misery
And I still had two more tests
In Chemistry and Filipino
Truly, misery begets company

All this pressure made me weep
And I was so stressed out

My tests turned into nightmares
Chasing me even into my sleep

Until that momentous Thursday
I switched on my laptop
Stared, breathed, hyperventilated
And fainted dead away

DANNY MESSER HALF-NAKED
Those arms, those abs, that pelvic V
Oh god, was there ever such a man
Who looked so sacred

I don't care if I'm half his age
In today's modern world
When it comes to true love
Age just isn't the gauge

Thank you to the powers that be
Just when I thought my sanity was lost to me
You had to send half-naked Danny
To rescue poor little me

DANNY HALF-NAKED saved my week
And that for now
Will be the short to-be continued story
Of my life, so to speak

Until the time when the writers hear
Of my plea to just bare some more
Then I shall jubilantly jump and squeal
DANNY ALL-NAKED saved my year!

The Shadow Of Her Passing

The chill breeze flutters the drapes in the drawing room
Stirring the ashes in the darkened gloom

Pale moonlight bathes the man
Bringing to light the cane held by the trembling hand

The broad back which has now begun to stoop
And the lined face on his chest slowly droops

But it is his eyes, sunken and red-rimmed
Burning with a feverish light, oddly undimmed

It has been but a week
But already her presence he seeks

In the way she opened the door
And the rustle of her skirts on the rosewood floor

How candlelight gleamed upon her laughing face
And the waltz she danced with such grace

The pansy eyes of such vivid hue
And the smiling mouth curved in a roue

He yearned to have her sweet form by his side
The soft curls on his chest reside

How swift the hand of death had struck
Everything came to a halt, abrupt

The faded eyes fill with tears
Even now, alone, he could sense her near

The many years they had together
He was selfish to want her forever

Perhaps to tell her again he loved her most
How without her, he was so lost

To cherish the look of love upon her face
And the warmth of her tender embrace

That she had been his breath, his life
Her passing cutting deep like a knife

How he missed her, this gnawing emptiness
Intruding into slumber, giving him no rest

His tears, like the river, flow
Unheeded to the stone-cold floor below

This pain will cease when comes Death
When with a gasp, he draws his last breath

Till then, each day shall break into tomorrow
And parting will always be sweet sorrow.

I Walked Into A Crumbling Keep

The wind soughs through the trees
At night
The branches powerless against
Its stormy might

The leaves struggle not
To fall
Clinging tightly with outstretched arms
Hoping their inevitable demise to forestall

It sweeps none too gently into
The crumbling keep
Stirring dead ashes into the
Blackened deep

Tattered tapestries of forest scenes
From a time long past
Slowly unfurl like a canvas
Upon a ship's mast

The wind flitters slowly now to the
Grave carved in stone
Where the weeping angels lay their heads
Above the covered pile of bones

A melody as if from a distant harp
Begins to play
Echoing through the silent ruins
The lilting music so light and gay

Light suffuses the aged keep
The strike of matches against the tallow
Luminescence chasing
The black and forbidding shadows

The lord and the lady have arisen
From their sleep
In the light of the glowing moon
Their hearts will again meet

She in her raiment of
Glowing white
Clothed in the colors
Of her shining knight

He stands with the claymore by
His side
Her hand resting in his
Adoring love in her eyes reside

From where they walk
The keep has sprang to life
Returning to its glory days
Of his love, his wife

A long and rousing cheer
From those long dead
Reminiscent of that time
When they had been newly wed

Petals lay scattered upon the
Rush-strewn floor
Kerchiefs of white fluttering
From every door

What a time it must
Have been
As I stared before me at
The unfolding scene

The wind once again blew through
The keep
And slowly the people headed back
For their eternal sleep

In the now-quiet graveyard
Where the stone angels weep
The lord and his lady
Took their last step

The rosy fingers of dawn had come
To reach
Into every nook and cranny of the crumbling keep
It sought to breach

Slowly I read the inscription on
The gravestone
The words etched deep
Their meaning touching home

Life and Death are but
Mortality
But Love in its purest form
Eternity transcending Mortality.

Heiress

All I wanted was love
But a gold crib I was laid in instead
Silver rattles for my tiny hands
But never the scent of my mother's touch

All I wanted was love
The finest toys to call my own
Nannies at my beck and call
The vast emptiness of it all

All I wanted was love
Wonderful balls and splendid gowns
The farce of a laugh
To mask an anguished heart

All I wanted was love
Beaus by the droves
Tiffany's, roses, and champagne
Fleeting and without meaning

All I wanted was love
Husbands loving my money more
Tabloids and gossip keeping score
What price to pay for Love?

All I wanted was love
Shallow, pretentious friends
No child to give me joy
Sleepless are my nights

All I wanted was love
Near my end
It haunts me still
My hopeful heart cannot forsake

All I wanted was love
Was it ever too much to ask?
A handful of emeralds I would give
To live a Life.

The Lady Of Glenymere Isle

In the worn pages of History
She is known as the Lady of Glenymere Isle

Glenymere Isle, where the diving terns and the
Crashing surf pound against the weathered rocks

But to us born of her seed
She is Lady Madeleine, most beloved of Glenymere

Her ebony hair of deepest velvet night
Sapphire eyes reflecting the turbulent seas

Her Beauty sighed upon by men
Of bold spirit and courageous heart

But deep sadness inside her wells
Discord melody springs from her flute

Many are the nights she wanders alone
Gazing out the cliff; seeing what cannot be seen

Her people grieve to see her so
Helpless against her pain

Betrayed by the one she loved
Seeking the love of another

Her heart left an open wound
No salve to the festering sore

Into this darkness came Tristan
Mighty lord from the north

Held captive by her winsomeness
Caught by her unrelenting pain

Lady Madeleine confused at her scattered thoughts
His nearness resurrecting things long dead

Coaxing a smile from her sweet lips
A trickle of laughter from the barren gloom

Her eyes alive with Life
Her heart beating like the fluttering tern

His love warmed her like the sun
Madeleine unfurled to bask in his glow

He was Spring to her Winter
The balm to her pain

No longer would she walk in Autumn alone
Moored to Tristan against the windswept rocks

Many the nights they walked as one
Seeing what with lovers' eyes can be seen

From within, Joy and Love overflow
Her cup filled beyond its brim

Her feet light upon the path
Melodious strains upon the flute

To those whom she remains unknown
She is merely the Lady of Glenymere Isle

But to us whom her love bore fruit
She is Most Beloved Madeleine
The Joy of her People and the
Keeper of his Heart.

Blood Upon The Snow

She stands still
A forlorn figure in gray
The drabness of her cloak
Echoing the night's lonely chill

The hood falls
A face young for its years
Yet etched deep in the darkened eyes
Lurking shadows of unfathomable pain

The white hands grip
Bloodless in their strength
A single, wilted red rose
Its brittle petals brave against the frigid winds

The quaking of her shoulders
The falling snow pays no heed
Salty rivulets down sooty lashes
Fall, uneased unto the unforgiving ground

Seeking the memory of his face
The warmth of his touch
The coldness, the isolation
Reaching deep in her very core

His fervent promises dwindling to a dying fire
Doused by the fearsome storm
The very lightness of his words
Swept like dead leaves without weight

Trampling upon her heart
Imprints of contempt laying waste
Leaving her barren to her very depths
Clutching on the fringes of hope

Scarlet is the blood
That drips against the pristine white
The curved thorns gouging deep
Like the talons cutting into her heart

The petals fall softly
Awash in tears and trails of red
The forlorn figure in gray, a picture
Of blood upon the snow.

Aloneness

I have only my muted heart, no words to speak
For so long from me, Love has chosen not to seek

My hands restless to lay upon my lover's hair
Shadowed eyes of yearning stares

The night whispers hang empty, devoid and bare
Flighty, passing without a care

My feet, chastened in their aloneness
My embrace, filled with loneliness

The painful throbbing echoes at night
For her, for Love that is out of sight

Years it has been
And yet the longing is still keen

Still my heart brims with hope
Perhaps Love's fire it can still stoke

Though Time's chances may be far and few
If Fate only knew

To this muted heart, give a moment's respite
A brief moment, to end the interminable night

A grasp of joy and a trickle of laughter
And perhaps, the dream of a happy ever after.

To My Beloved

Oh, but to see her lovely face
Tranquil in its repose
Or perched upon her arm
The glorious profile
Upturned to the kisses of the sun

Oh, but to see her lovely face
Her eyes of infinite love
Resting upon the beloved
Tenderly caressing like
The gentle wind upon the austere moor

Oh, but to see her lovely face
A hint of rouge on the youthful cheeks
Peony-red stains upon creamy skin
Vibrant and abloom
A bud awakening to the touch of Spring

Oh, but to see her lovely face
Petal-soft lips lingering of
Harvest's sweetest wine
A kiss of bliss
Of love truly divine

Oh, but to see her lovely face
And know that her heart beats for me, oh mortal man
This precious treasure I hold
My lips upon her scented brow
My Beloved, the very reason of my heart.

A Place In The Sun

I watch the past unfold
The gray shadows slowly unfurl
The hard days and the despair-filled nights
When Happiness was but a drop in a bitter brew

How stark! How cold!
The only life I knew
Laughter was ever so far
And Hunger constantly beside

But still I stood bold
Unbowed before the winds of Fate
Courage set my stride
And Purpose placed me on high

By suffering I was mold
These hands of toil and grime
Mud-caked feet steadfastly stood
Charting the forbidding skies

The glimmer of gold
Like the shimmering tear in my eye
Harvest of bounty
Gleaned upon the favorable earth

The future is mine to hold
Where this dream once seemed so far
So surely now it walks with me
Favored son of Fate.

You Are My Spring

You are my Spring
To this heart, long cloaked in Winter

You are my Spring
Bringing colored hues to a palette of gray

You are my Spring
Your coming has been my awakening

You are my Spring
Your constant love, a beacon in the tempestuous gales

You are my Spring
Your wondrous caring, a balm to my afflictions

You are my Spring
 Your embrace where I find my solace

You are my Spring
Your gentle understanding has been my strength

You are my Spring
Your presence the bringer of my joy

You are my Spring
And my one true love.

The Story Of Lizzie Borden

The town of Fall River has never been the same
It's always known with macabre recall made famous by the Borden name

The address was Number Ninety two, Second Street
The fourth day of August, in the sweltering summer heat

Mr. Andrew Jackson Borden was found dead
On a couch in the sitting room his corpse was spread

And the one who found him, the daughter who shared his name
Lizzie Borden, who was later to take the blame

Who could have done such a hideous deed
In this quiet, peaceful town, who indeed

But that was not all for in the guest bedroom they found
The bloodied body of Abby Borden, lying on the ground

She had been killed first, so it seemed
And the murderer then attacked her husband, unseen

Only Lizzie and Bridget, the maid, were in the house that day
For Emma Borden, the elder sister, had gone visiting away

Could someone have crept in while they were all unaware
And done away with the Bordens beneath the sun's unforgiving stare

Could it have been Bridget, the maid, gone mad
For being asked to wash windows when the summer heat was so bad?

Or could it have been church-going, respectable, spinsterly Lizzie
Could her father's plan to change his will drive her to a murderous frenzy?

It's true, she had never loved Abby as her mother
The loss of a maternal bosom could never be replaced by another

She was the one with the most motive
At the funeral, she was the one with no tears to give

On these murder charges she was sent to plead
And yet many people couldn't believe a woman capable of this heinous deed

"I am innocent," was all she had to say
While the jury deliberated on her future, come what may

After a very brief fourteen days
A verdict of "Not Guilty" was handed down that June day

Ostracized by the town, Lizzie sought to build her life again
Living at Maplecroft, that gray Victorian house, till she was at life's end

But even after her death, the stories have refused to die
Some branding her trial and acquittal an outright lie

What secrets she may have harbored, we will never know
Carried down into her grave, deep, deep below

But in most of our minds, this image will always stand
Lizzie Borden, hatchet in hand, under the sweltering sun.

The Long Wait

I stare out the window
At the wind, filtering through the trees
How mournful she blows

The trees with their souls laid bare
Facing the onslaught of autumn
She, with her unforgiving stare

The birds have left for other parts to call
And still I wait for you,
For not even a letter has come at all

Wasn't it only last Spring
When you bade me goodbye
Even then, was it just a fling?

You told me to wait for you
Saying you'd come back for me
That your love was true

And now that seasons have passed
My heart trembles in fear
Was this a love to last?

I hasten to brush away the tears
In my unguarded moments
I long to still my fears

Even now, I long for your embrace
To hear your voice, to see the sun
Shining upon that beloved face

Winter will soon be here
The trees will be barren then
And I will be waiting, still.

The First Time I'm Going To Say I Love You

I know now that what they say is true
That when you're meant for love, it will come to you

In the most unexpected of times
And sometimes in the most unlikely places

For quite some time, my heart hadn't been in it
It would be untrue to say that I hadn't been hurt more than a bit

So when the call came, I was very surprised
Too late to change my mind, I realized

It was just like high school, getting to know you
Talking about things, as silly as why the sky is colored blue

I cannot quite say how I feel when the phone rings
Except that to me it is the most wonderful thing

I secretly cherish the seemingly nonsensical things you say
Like how am I doing and how was my day

On the first day that we were to meet
I couldn't understand the trembling that I felt

Or why the laughter came so easily this time
And why our thoughts seemed to be in rhyme

I couldn't sleep well that night
Thoughts of you were always in sight

I couldn't begin to put into words how I felt about you
Except that somehow I knew all of this was true

I feel safe and cherished with you
And might I say, loved by you, too?

This courting stage, this period of discovering
We both know where this is leading

I have always been one to hide my feelings
Because there has never been someone who was my everything

I have never said the words before
Never had someone to say them to

I love you
My very first time to say these words

I have never felt this way about anyone before
And I will say it again and again
Because it is true, I really do love you.

The Days Of Fall

Do you remember the beauty of Fall?
Do you remember those beautiful days at all?

How we raced beneath the trees, lonely and bare
How young we were then, free without a care

The leaves in hues of gold, brown, and amber
The look in your eyes, warmly glowing embers

We smiled at the look on each other's faces
We saw how Love had left its traces

How we walked hand in hand
How beneath the swirling leaves we would stand

Do you remember those days at all?
Do you remember the wonder that was Fall?

I look at you and I know you do remember
I look at those same warmly glowing embers

I know you cherish our love
I know you think of those days with the leaves swirling above

You always hold me by the hand
You and I would always stand

In the one place where we were the happiest
In the one place where our days were endless

I see you with the gentle lines of Love on your face
I see how the passing years have left their trace

You touch my silvery hair and the fading gold band
You gently take my fragile hand

And you tell me you remember those wondrous days of Fall
And you tell me those were the most beautiful days of all.

Solitary

I gaze at the stars blanketing the sky
Their silent stares asking me why

I hear the wind as she passes me unseen
She longs to ask where I have been

The scent of the night fills me within
As never in his arms I had been

I taste the tears upon my cheek
Salty trails running down in streaks

My hands are numb and cold
Away from his warm, strong hold

Here I am alone, in the vast black night
He, whom my world once revolved in, nowhere in sight

And it is I, left to pine for a love once had and lost
Like Spring yearning for the end of Winter's frost

With only sad memories and broken dreams
And my falling tears a steady stream.

Shattered

Today you came
And broke my heart
Standing there
I heard the words falling from your lips

I stood so quietly
My very heart shattered
My hands, frozen, where they trembled
Against my sides

You didn't look at me
How could you say you're sorry
When your body turns away from me
Your heart, that you had given to someone else

Did I ever love this face
How could I have given you my love
You never once touched my face
How could you not see my tears

Have our memories vanished
Have I been that fleeting to you
Have you forgotten me completely
This girl, standing in front of you

Asking you, beseeching you
Not to hurt her like this
This wrenching, tearing pain
How could you be this heartless

You do not see me
That much I can see in your eyes
She has erased my touch
But it's you who have betrayed me

Betrayed me and my love for you
And still you say you're sorry
You do not wait for my words
And start walking away

Leaving me alone to weep
The stabbing, piercing pain
It leaves me incoherent
Is this how dying feels?

You walk away, farther still
Today you came
And broke my heart.

Rain

Rain,
Come down on me tonight
Come and wash this pain
Sweep it out of sight

Rain,
Fall upon this troubled heart
Fall gently on my misery
Be a friend and play your part

Rain,
The night has gone on for so long
The stars only stare piteously
Only your presence, I have sought all along

Rain,
Only you can heal this ache
Only you know so well the despairing grief
My hurt and my tears, please take

Rain,
In my solitude, do not leave me
In my loneliness, keep close
Don't just let me be

Rain,
Do let this heart live again
Do let this night not be forever
Rain, Rain, I shall wait for you then.

Mercedes Of Orleans

Her name was Maria de las Mercedes of Orleans
And her birthplace was the Palacio Real in Madrid, Spain

She was destined to be his one true love
And yet none knew of Fate's plan to thwart them from above

She grew up in the bosom of her large family
Young and carefree, seemingly unmarred by tragedy

Princess as she was, she, too, had her share of grief
A beloved brother and sister, whose lives were too brief

During this tumultuous time, her aunt, the Queen of Spain was deposed
Her rule the Spanish people strongly opposed

And it was in this time of exile when Mercedes first met
The man whom she would love until the twilight set

How her young heart must have stirred at the sight
Alfonso, the Prince of Asturias, filled her dreamy nights

Her blossoming love, to her great joy was requited
The Prince, in her loving ways he delighted

They were engaged on a beautiful December night
Surely, only happiness and joy wished upon the lovely sight

Marriage bells soon tolled for the starry pair
Both of them, of the grief soon to befall them, so unaware

So soon her health began to fail
And the king, beside his adored, so strained and pale

Tuberculosis in those days had no cure
Desperate, her pain and suffering he had to endure

Till she slipped away into eternal rest
Leaving Alfonso to grieve alone, he who had loved her best

Soon he had to marry again, for Spain and its throne
Of this loveless marriage, an heir was born

But for the short life that was to be his
Alfonso would be forever tormented by that time of bliss

And he would have welcomed Death when it came
Perhaps even calling his beloved's name

And Mercedes, she who had been his love, his life
Would have walked with him into the gentle night

Celebrating in death the love they were denied in life.

When Death Has Parted Us

I lie alone in the shuttered room
My grief echoed by the darkening gloom

Has it just been mere days
When everything I loved was taken away?

And yet Time has passed by so slowly
Its unhurried pace a bane to my melancholy

With you gone, everything has ceased for me
The beauty outside, my eyes have failed to see

Beauty means nothing to me
Without you beside me, nothing will ever be

I long only for you
My one love so true

But you are forever lost to me
And this grief I know will remain to be

I yearn for you, deeply
Your passing I feel most strongly

And yet, I still feel you near
And though I know you cannot hear

I want to tell you once again
That you are and always have been
My one love till the very end.

How Long Have You Waited?

How long have you waited?
I didn't see the shadows darkening your eyes.

How long have you waited?
I never saw the droop to the sweet mouth.

How long have you waited?
I didn't hear the yearning in your voice.

How long have you waited?
I never heard the beating of your lonely heart.

How long have you waited?
I didn't know that Love had held itself from you.

How long have you waited?
I never knew of the silent tears at night.

How long have you waited?
I didn't know of the dashed hopes and broken dreams.

How long have you waited?
I never knew of your sorrowing pain.

But now, I have come to know them all
Come, let me love you.

Let me hold you
Rest your heart against mine.

I know you waited a long time
But the wait is now over.

I am here
I am here to love you forever.

From Laura, With Love

On the day that I was born
Dawn was just about to break into morn

There I was, a tiny bundle swathed in pink
Sharing in my parents' love, a precious link

It was supposed to be a story with a happy ending
Instead, it was the start of a very different beginning

There were the chills, the night sweats; weakness and fatigue set in
My parents were confused, the doctors baffled; where to begin

The countless hospital visits and painful blood tests
How I wanted it to stop, just to rest

I just wanted to be a twelve year old girl
Doing as girls do and imagining thoughts of that first twirl

When I saw my parents crying, on that day I came home
Deep inside I knew that bad news had to be borne

My white blood cells were multiplying much too fast, much too much
My body just couldn't cope with such

I remember crying way into the night
Why, why was God keeping out of sight?

My family and friends were quick to embrace me
Stilling my despairing heart with words of comfort as they wept with me

As time passed, my denials did give way to acceptance
With such odds against me, I decided to take a courageous stance

The journey has been full of bumps and curves
Sometimes we didn't know what faced us as we took a swerve

There were times when I felt worst and sometimes when I felt my best
To race for a cure, nobody would give that matter rest

I once asked my mother why God had chosen me
And she said that some things are just meant to be

That maybe God was missing me so much in heaven
And wanted His angel with him in His safe haven

That He never gives trials that He knows we cannot overcome
Hoping through them, better persons we might become

And that quieted my heart, comforted me as nothing ever had
And mother, seeing my understanding, was so glad

I know that my time is short; it might come too soon—that day
So to everyone I have ever known, these words I have to say

To my mother and father, thank you for the time, the love, and the care
This has never been any secret, but still I'd like to lay the words bare

To my brothers and sisters, for the understanding, love, and happy moments
Having you with me has eased the pain and torment

My relatives, who by a phone call or with a visit
Perked me up in those times when I was weakest in spirit

My friends, who have loved me and laughed with me through those days
My heart is overwhelmed by your friendship, is all that I can say

The doctors and nurses with their diligent care and healing hands
My defenders, always with me taking the stand

To God, for the precious and blessed life I was given
How comforting to know that I will soon be with Him in heaven

Forgive me, then, if I always seemed to be chasing after time
For one such as me, that is the gift of the divine

Or if I was too avid, grasping even, in making memories
I just wanted to take part in everyone's stories

Cry if you must but do not be sad for very long
I will be in His arms, where I have always belonged

Be happy, because I will be, twirling to that familiar refrain
A beautiful life, unmarred by pain

So before I fade away into the endless night
Before my sweet goodbyes echo out of sight

I ask God to grant me this last request
I know He will not deny, for He loves me best

To let me die just like the day I was born
When Dawn is about to break into a beautiful morn.

Do You Know How It Feels To Be Loved?

Do you know how it feels to be loved?
Each morning is bright with promise.

Do you know how it feels to be loved?
It is there in the whisper of the morning mist.

Do you know how it feels to be loved?
The stars tremble against the darkening sky.

Do you know how it feels to be loved?
The gentle wind sighs as she passes by.

Do you know how it feels to be loved?
The nights are tender in their darkness.

Do you know how it feels to be loved?
Dawn is resplendent in her loveliness.

Do you know how it feels to be loved?
The frolicking sea meets the shore in a rush.

Do you know how it feels to be loved?
The roses bow their heads with a blush.

Do you know how it feels to be loved?
I know, because I am loved by you.

A Visit From Winter

She came in the dark of night
Her frosty breath extinguishing all light

Her wind-frozen robes swept outside the door
Raining icicles and snow on the wooden floor

I looked at her and knew
What my heart had known for sometime was true

What she told me with her eyes
Was truth which I had tried to disguise

When she spoke, her voice was winter-mist
And what she said was this:

"I could not bear to see you pining and all
So tonight I have come to call,"

"You must know how he betrayed your heart
You never meant as much, even from the start,"

"Weep if you must for that is the truth
Your torrent of tears will help to soothe,"

"I have nothing but Time to salve your pain
And Hope that your next love won't be in vain."

With her icy hold she took my hands
Her compassionate gaze willing me to understand

That I was not at fault, never had been
That Love can be cruel at times, it seems

With a last touch of my face, she left
Her departure leaving me numb and bereft

And I watched her from where I lay in bed
Seeing Winter riding away in her imperial sled.

Danny And Lindsay: A Love Story

(inspired by the television series, CSI NY)

We first met at the zoo
I said, "How you doin'?"
And you smiled at me, too.

Montana, my name for you
The stolen glances I send your way
Are those not enough clues?

I find myself intrigued by you
A slip of a country girl who always
Had so much work to do.

Never time for some dinner or drinks
How many times have I asked you
I cannot anymore think.

Your hand in mine, a perfect fit
I saw in the way you didn't linger
It unsettled you more than just a bit.

What dark secrets lie behind your eyes
When I get too near, a chasm of reserve
Between us you cannot disguise.

But I have seen you lighthearted and free
Relaxed and happy, a different person
You are a sight to see.

Bug dinners, down time at Cosy's
Me carrying you
We are good together, everyone agrees.

When I hold you against me
My lips against your hair, right next to my heart
The only place where you should be.

You like me that much, you said
But now is not the time, too much left undone
Too many things left unsaid.

Something scarred you in the past
It plagues and haunts you still
But with time, these things will not last.

Will you not let me in
Perhaps together we can overcome the
Pain and anguish raging within.

But I take heart in the things you say
What I have for you, this feeling is true
I believe love will find its way.

If you need me, I will be near
I will calm and comfort your fears
And when you decide the time to love is
Now, I will be here.

Part 3

AND THEN SOME ESSAYS

To My White Knight

When I was young, I always dreamt that someday a white knight would come galloping by on his handsome steed, and take me off to live with him in his shining castle. I would lie down on my bed and hold the book of fairytales close to my chest, dreaming of that day when he would come. I held on to that dream for many years, even when I left the little girl with the pigtails behind. Even when there was nobody to turn the yellowed pages of the worn fairytale book.

Love called to me and I answered each time believing and hoping for the best. But it would turn out to be just another infatuation or an instance of unrequited love. It would leave my untried heart bruised and bleeding; and it would always keep me wondering if perhaps, I was wrong to believe that there would be someone in this world for me. Maybe I placed too strong a belief in my white knight, and so little by little, the dream faded away. I distanced myself from my girlish yearnings, my romantic notions, and my sentimental heart. I taught myself to be pragmatic and realistic. No longer did I look down the road for a glimpse of someone riding by. The trail became covered with dust; and ivy vines soon twined itself around my heart, making the way almost impassable. My heart thudded with life but its beating was a forlorn sound, loneliness echoing in its very depths.

You changed all that. Into that dusty trail came a set of footprints, imprints which never wavered with the strong winds, and never receded with the ebbing of the tide. It frightened and confused me, awakening emotions I thought had long been buried. It unsettled me greatly that you stirred these feelings within me, for I had no wish to encounter love. As far as I had come to know it, my life was perfect. Perhaps too serenely placid; but I liked it that way, no waves to shatter the smooth surface. But the more I resisted, the deeper the footprints dug into the dusty trail. I decided to be brave and meet you. I was prepared to be hurt but not to be surprised.

You crept into my heart, slowly. You drew me out; you showed me that it was safe to walk the path again, which had given me much pain and despair. It was in the way we talked, in the many hours you spent getting to know me better. I could hear it in your voice, in the way you laughed, and I saw it in the way your eyes held mine. The gentleness and the love I saw beckoned to something deep inside of me; and for the first time in many years, I opened my heart once again. I was prepared for whatever would come from that, but instinctively, I knew there was something different this time. It was there in the quickening of my pulse, in the radiance of my smile, and the love songs in my heart. You made my old yearnings come alive, and I began to grasp with eager fingers at the remnants of my childhood dream. And after so long a time, that night I opened the yellowed book again, and fell asleep holding it close to my chest.

I love you. Do you know how long I have waited to say the words? I truly do. Where before my heart was frozen in the clutches of winter, you have thawed it with the warmth and brilliance of spring. You have touched my heart in its innermost recesses and given it cause to bloom. I look at life differently, and I live it differently because of you. I realize how glorious the daffodils are in the fields. How solemnly lovely it is to walk in the gathering twilight with the fireflies dancing around our heads. How wonderful it is to laugh aloud with sheer joy. Your love has unveiled the true me, the one I kept hidden all these years beneath a stoic and hardened heart. I cannot even begin to remember how I had lived that way for all that time. With you

I can share my darkest sorrows and the most painful secrets; and you with your characteristic tenderness would enfold me in your arms, until my tears had dried upon your sleeve. You keep my fears and worries at bay with your steadfast love. In this world where storms lash out at the most frail of crafts; you anchor me closely to your side, protecting me from the buffeting winds. My heart will always be in your keeping.

    I look at the trail and I see that the dust has vanished. The vines around my heart have long loosened their grip, and the path is filled with light. And I can see the two sets of footprints, firmly entrenched and so close side by side. I couldn't have asked for anyone but you. Truly, my white knight has come and he has saved me with the gift of his love.

Walking In The Rain

It is going to rain, Kate. I can feel it. The clouds have been slowly gathering all afternoon. Now they hang in misshapen clusters of leaden gray. The wind has picked up, hastening the fragile leaves' descent down the busy avenue. Everywhere the air is heavy with the scent of ripened rain. I breathe it in and revel in its earthy richness. The rain brought me you, Kate.

It had been an afternoon such as this. I was hurrying from work, just like the others, not wanting to get caught in the downpour that had been threatening all day. The first fat drops spattered on the concrete road, and I raised my face to see the sky unleashing its pent-up fury. Umbrellas popped up like little doll houses; the colors and prints clashing with one another as their owners scurried for cover. There was a break in the crowd and I quickly darted in, hoping to make my way to the little café on the corner before the rain completely soaked me. I hit something and suddenly we were sprawled on the street, multicolored jelly beans and candy sprinkles flying in every direction. I looked down, into the prettiest face I had ever seen, framing a pair of laughing eyes. Your eyes caught me, held me, so that I didn't mind that people were looking admiringly at the pretty picture we made. The wind suddenly blew your umbrella away and I chased after it, wondering at the woman who carried the Dalmatian-printed umbrella.

We had piping hot coffee in that little café, and I offered to buy you the little tea cakes with their brilliant streaks of icing. It was the least I could do after smashing your jellybean and candy sprinkle jars. You love color, that much I knew. The yellow scarf and the apple-green suit said as much. I could see the way your eyes roved lovingly over the pastel-hued scones and the rainbow-colored jam tarts. I knew then that you were extraordinary, Kate. And then you started to talk about rain. And I found myself wishing that the rain would never stop, so that we could stay all afternoon in that cozy café. And I could lose myself in the merry pools of blue that held so much warmth and laughter.

You love the rain. Always have. The scent it brings, the promise of something wonderful just hearing the pitter patter of the falling drops, and watching the angry thunderclouds grumbling above. The way you love to step your shoes into the puddles, just to see how far they would sink, and then shrieking with laughter as a passing car sprayed you with rain water. How rain brings newness to everything it touches, unfurling the shy petals of a bud, and coaxing birth from the parched and barren ground. You saw the world in a sea of colored umbrellas and made a game of pointing out the most distinctive ones. Umbrellas should have personality, you said. But walking in the rain was what you loved most, watching your footsteps vanish in the liquid swirls and gazing at everything through sheets of falling water. The world looks different through the rain, you told me.

I had never thought of rain as beautiful before I met you, Kate. You colored my life the way you colored yours. With rain. I like it that you have an assortment of umbrellas for almost every rainy day that is sure to come down on us. There's the one with the pink hearts which we took with us on our first Valentine's Day date. Then there is the plaid one which makes us feel very Burberry-English indeed. Then one of my favorite ones, the one with the painted ducks all over. We took it wading with us in the pond and made quacking noises just for laughs. There's the black one which we used to dance ala Gene Kelly in Singing In The Rain. Many couples ended up following suit and we had a most memorable day. Or the one with all the teapots which we always take with us whenever we visit our favorite café. But I love walking alone with you best of all, Kate. Putting my arm around you and loving the feel of your head upon my shoulder. I like your love encompassing me in the steadily falling rain. You raise your face up to me, and I see the tiny beads of moisture dotting your hair, making it sparkle like silver. I brush my hand against it, and the look in your eyes makes my breath halt in overflowing tenderness. I see the rain and my world differently because of you, Kate. And it is truly beautiful.

The rain is starting to come down. I laugh aloud with sheer joy and open my arms to catch the scattering drops. I pull my coat tighter around me and open my umbrella. Ginger-colored cats dancing against a blue background. Walk with me, Kate. Walk with me in the rain forever.

Dear Gerty

(The first love letter of Samuel Tristan Cooper to Alexandra Gertrude Travis)

Dear Gerty,

I wonder what you are doing tonight. As for me, I am sitting at my desk writing a letter. It's for you, of course. The moon is out and there are lots of stars dotting the inky black sky. Can you see it from your desk, Gerty? I wish we could watch it together. There! Did you see that? The Big Dipper and the Little Dipper beside it. You taught me to look for constellations, remember? Funny how but those two suddenly remind me of us two. Sam and Gerty.

I like you, Gerty. I always have. I can still recall the first day we met. I was standing at the bus stop waiting for Old Yellow to drive up the lane when I heard a squeaking noise. I looked up the street to see you walking towards me, the prettiest face with a shy smile under a fringe of light brown bangs, wearing the shiniest pair of red Mary Janes I had ever seen. I couldn't help but smile back and breathe a smile of relief. Somebody was making noise, too! You with your squeaky new shoes and I with my rattling lunchbox. We looked adorable together. I know because mom took a first-day-of-school-picture. The red Mary Janes and the new, rattling lunchbox shining for all the world to see.

You're one of the best students in class. Our adviser, Miss Hodgkins, says so. That makes me like you more. Especially when you help me with all those commas and apostrophes. Sometimes I still can't figure out which is which. Well, it's rather natural that girls are better at English. My mom said that and of course, she's a girl, just an older girl. You're a real trooper, too, Gerty. For all the times I've seen you always wearing dresses, I would never have thought that you would dare hold a frog in Science class. Boy! Did Winifred Peters turn as green as her frog! But you, you were so nonchalant about it, stroking it like it was a pet dog! I think that's why the girls elected you as group leader.

I don't know why I suddenly feel like writing to you tonight, Gerty. It's the first time I have written a letter to a girl. I just want you to know that I like you very much. All the boys in class like you, too. I wish I could sock all of them in the nose. I hope you don't like them too much. I wouldn't want to be sent to detention for causing a nosebleed. I always look forward to Saturdays. You may not notice it, but I always search the bleachers for you while I'm standing on the pitcher's mound. I play better when you are there wildly cheering and yelling. Remember the time when you had the mumps and couldn't go see the Little League play? I didn't even make a home run that day! But when the next Saturday came by, I played ball with a vengeance, and we took home the Little Leaguers' Trophy. You were beaming from ear to ear and your face was flushed. Your poster read go, Sam, go!

I like any excuse to hold your hand. It makes my heart want to burst. I like looking after you, too. Whether we are crossing the street, playing in the stream, or going to the corner store for candy. I always save a little of my pocket money so that I can buy you some of those pink-striped lollipops that you like so much. I like to see you smile and laugh. It's contagious. I hope I got the spelling right and the apostrophe, too. You have always been very pretty. The long brown hair, the sparkling brown eyes, and the pearly-white smile. I sometimes don't know what to say anymore. You make my stomach do flip-flops, something which our gym teacher, Miss Crane, could never make me do. Of course, she is nowhere as pretty as you.

I think I love you, Gerty. You make me think of sunshiny days and sugar-coated cookies. You are light, laughter, and caring. Sorry, I can't be Elizabeth Barrett Browning. You're the one who taught me about constellations, and now I love to gaze at them as much as you do. Being with you makes me happy. Our English play will be tomorrow. I am very happy to be playing the part of Prince Charming because I get to kiss you at the end, and I wouldn't have to worry about it one bit because it's all part of the script. This is an awfully long letter. Miss Hodgkins would be very pleased to know that her efforts at teaching us letter-writing are bearing fruit. Someday I will give you this letter, Gerty. Goodnight now. This knight needs a good night's sleep to banish the evil dragon tomorrow.

Love,

Sam (who is twelve years old)

P.S. I will marry you someday, Gerty. Scout's honor.

Dear Sam

(The first love letter of Alexandra Gertrude Travis to Samuel Tristan Cooper)

Dear Sam,

It is a beautiful night tonight. The moon is so bright and the constellations are all out there. It's almost as if they came out to join the parade. I think it's because they know that we will be staging our first-ever English play tomorrow and have come to wish us good luck. I wore my gown again just a few minutes ago and twirled in front of the mirror. That's a secret we girls never tell you boys, but I'm letting you in on it because I know you won't tease me about it. Our big day tomorrow. Day. What a funny word to enter my mind just now.

Do you remember the day we met? It was a Monday, the first day of school. I was so embarrassed because my red Mary Janes, which I really loved, were so noisy, squeaky in their newness. Then I saw you, neat and handsome in your new shirt and trousers, trying to steady your shiny lunchbox to stop its rattling. That's when I knew that we were going to be good friends. You held my hand real tight and side by side we waited for the bus to drive up the lane. Samuel Tristan Cooper and Alexandra Gertrude Travis. We were the shiniest pair that day.

I voted for you for class president, not that it would matter anyhow. The whole class voted for you, except for George Cambert and Kevin Bridges because they were absent that day. You proudly stood up and made your speech. The whole class was rigid with attention and we gave you a standing ovation.

Even Miss Hodgkins was teary-eyed over it. She was really so affected by it she didn't give us homework that weekend. Maybe you should be an actor, Sam. That's a great idea and I could be your tutor making sure that you get your punctuation marks correct. I really like you, Sam. Of course, it helps that you're handsome. Black hair and the nicest pair of gray eyes. Last December, I overheard Melissa Ames talking with her friends in the girls' bathroom. Now, that apostrophe is correct. She said your eyes make her melt like chocolate. I remembered thinking that you would think it silly, too, as it was winter and nothing melts in winter!

You're the best in scouting, Sam. You've got all those badges to show. I remember your mom telling my mom how glad she was that you knew how to cook, so that she won't have to worry about you starving to death. Wow, it must really be a rarity that boys know how to cook! You play Little League very well, too. I always block out my Saturdays to watch you play. You're my favorite player, Sam, and I'm not just saying that because we're friends. Even Coach Barnes thinks it, too. The way he talks about you, one would think you're Babe Ruth. Uh-huh. I can imagine him sitting in his office, your autographed posters papering his wall.

I am beginning to more than just like you, Sam. You know all those lollipops you have ever bought for me? I have kept all the wrappers. They rest at the bottom of my treasure box. Whenever I am with you I feel safe, cherished, and special. You don't tease me about the things I say or do, and you listen to even my most hare-brained ideas and the silliest stories. Remember the day I scraped my knee and you took me to the school clinic? You held my hand all throughout it and you were brave, so brave that I was embarrassed to cry. I like you holding my hand. And I like it even better because you don't do that to the other girls. I don't think I'd ever want to talk to you again if that happens.

I think I love you, Sam. I must because just the other day, I overheard Winifred Peters telling her girlfriends that she hopes you will take her to the Seniors' Dance Night, which is still four years from now, and there was this funny ache in the region of my heart. It didn't go away for quite a few days. I hope that you will take your best girl friend to the dance. She will save all her dances for you.

I am very glad that you will be playing Prince Charming tomorrow and that you have to kiss me so that I'll wake up from my hundred years' sleep. Here's another little secret. You're the first boy I have ever kissed, and even if we don't do it like they do in the movies, a kiss is still a kiss. I will hold my breath until it's time. Just don't take too long or I might turn blue. Goodnight, Sam. Don't forget to save me tomorrow.

Love,

Gerty (who will be twelve next week)

P.S. If you ask me to marry you, I will say yes.

The Promise

I have stood under the eaves for all these nameless nights, waiting. The moon, in her luminescence, has been a faithful companion, touching her silvery beams upon this solitary figure. I am grateful for her presence; it is always beautiful to have someone to walk with, someone who understands the depths of a sorrowing heart.

I shiver in the chill of the Autumn air. How fitting that Autumn should herald the coming of Winter, and that the changing of the seasons should see my love waning. In the trembling of the leaves, in the last moments before they fall, skittering and floating to their amber-gold graves, I see echoes of him.

The smile in his eyes and the laughter that came from his lips. I can remember the warmth of his touch, the clasp of his hand as the promise was made. I love you. I heard the beat of his heart as I lay nestled in his embrace. I love you. I saw my fingers, fragile and trembling, as I caressed his cheek. I love you. I heard it in the whisper of my lips, tremulous and soft. I love you. And the leaves fell all around us, touching, dancing, and swirling, encompassing us in the scent of love.

I love you. The night wind mocks me, delighting at the sight of my forlorn figure. She whispers his promises in my ear; empty words devoid of life, of feeling, as empty as her fingers unrelentingly cold upon my skin. I turn my shadowed eyes to her and the night wind ceases her play. Callous though she be, even she does not have the heart to stand before one whose eyes speak of stark pain.

He held my hands that day but his touch was cold, chillingly so. It seeped through me, cocooning me in a cold, numbing haze. I heard the beat of his heart but it was not for me. I tried to touch his cheek but he turned his face away. We were strangers in that place. And the leaves fell, mahogany-brown, darkest red, and amber-gold, floating and trembling, shushing my heart, willing it not to cry as his words rained with finality. He did not see the bewildered pain, could not comprehend the barrenness of the heart he had laid open. The tears never came; no tears could ever hope to assuage the agony. And I stood there while all around me, the leaves danced their paean of death.

I have wept my eyes dry. In the silence, the moon weeps along with me, weeping for a heart broken, for a heart betrayed. But she tells me, too, that the winter heart will not last forever. Heart be soothed, heart be still. Someone will come, someone worthy of my love. Until then in my pain, I must remember to nurture hope and love. And the moon will shine her luminescence on us, on the two figures standing under the eaves. And she will leave me, to walk with someone who understands the depths of a loving heart.

www.ingramcontent.com/pod-product-compliance
Lightning Source LLC
LaVergne TN
LVHW011930070526
838202LV00054B/4573